When Clouds Appear As Mountains

MALCOLM GILES

ISBN: 978-1-7349314-0-2

SKY PUDDLE INDUSTRIES

for more from the author, visit pocketbiome.com

I

Waiting is one of the worst things. It had already been a week, and it was the first week in a long time that I wasn't depressed. It felt like the first week of my life.

I never had a concrete reason for my depression. Mental health professionals were unable to find a cause, so they said I had a chemical imbalance in my brain. The introduction of a new chemical was making me question that. It became clear that the answer to the age-old question, "What do you want to be when you grow up?" was the source of my problems. I wanted to be an explorer, but was instead urged to choose a "real job." I never came up with another answer that I actually believed, but I still repressed the dream. Taking a first plateau dose of dextromethorphan made all that clear to me. The question had bothered me all those years because the answer had to be a job, and I never wanted to be a job.

I also started my first journal that wasn't somehow related to school that night. I used the first pages to plan a trip to the desert. I figured out all the logistics. Everything except for what I would do there, but I didn't want to plan that aspect of the trip. I was more interested in the journey, in exploring. It was like taking my first breath.

The experience left me curious about the second plateau. I had read a lot about dextromethorphan and its plateaus of effects. The first plateau was supposed to be a bit energetic and empathetic, something like MDMA, but with a dash more introspection. The second plateau was some strange realm of its own. The third was more dissociative, like ketamine. The fourth plateau was like the third but with contact from entities of some kind. The physical effects of the dissociative drug made it sound conducive to meditation. It seemed fool-hardy to dive into higher plateaus without experiencing the lower ones first. The second plateau had my interest in particular, as it sounded like a world between worlds. The substance wasn't all that popular because a lot of people found the trip unpleasant on any plateau. However, most people benefit from its antitussive properties in sub-psychedelic doses, so it was widely available in commercial cough medicine.

One week after my first experience, I had the house to myself. My mom was asleep and my brother was staying at his girlfriend's place. I poured a glass of thick, cherry-flavored liquid, twice as much as the first time, and brewed a cup of passion fruit tea to pair with the potion. I drank them both, smoked a bowl, went to my room, and put on some music.

Things grew strange after I sat down and closed my eyes. My body was gone, and I was staring into a jet black void. Colors began to pop into view, and soon they coalesced into a landscape. I fell into it.

I was wearing a long blue coat, standing atop a grassy hill, looking across a meadow. There was a city of concentric circles in the distance. Trying to get a closer look from the hill, I soon found myself inside the city, speaking to a black-haired woman. Something about her presence told me she was a priestess or some sort of magic woman. My attention turned towards my gloved hands. I was bewildered why I would be wearing gloves, my eyes opened and I was 18 in Ohio again.

I had no explanation for what had happened. I went into

the night believing that the five senses produced an accurate map of reality, but they no longer seemed like enough. It was like a waking dream, but it felt completely real. I had to be missing something. I decided the world had to be made of more than the sum of its parts, more than what my human mind could perceive. Everything was alive—the subjective experience was intrinsic to all matter. I closed my eyes again to try to get back to wherever I had been. Cognitive dissonances made themselves known. My interest in meditation was divorced from its history—I was trying to use an ancient spiritual practice for the sake of relaxation. I was drawn to spiritual practices but did not believe in spirits. I thought about this and drifted off into another sea of imagery. I saw myself in the third person. I was older and could finally grow a beard. I was laughing. I was with her. I heard her name for the first time.

"Fey."

I opened my eyes and got the notebook I had started on the first plateau. "Fey! She has to be real, somewhere," I wrote. "I saw her tonight, maybe it was a past life? Maybe it was the future? I don't know what to think anymore. But I've been dreaming of her for four years now. She must be out there, not just in my mind." I put down the notebook and picked up my electric guitar. It was a cheap Epiphone Les Paul, but it was my first guitar, and I had never named it. I decided to name it Fey and began to play.

I awoke the next day to find my revelations intact. The world seemed full of spirits, energy, and other realms. Fey was out there. And it seemed within my control to determine how things would unfold.

II

Patience wasn't getting any easier. Soon, I gave up on waiting every two weeks and settled on a routine of tripping once or twice a week. When I decided to graduate from high school early, I was planning on starting college early as well. I found out I wouldn't be able to get my financial aid until the fall, so I decided not to start college early. I had nothing but free time and essentially no one see. I applied to some jobs, but no one was particularly interested in the sort of short term work that I was looking for. I also didn't need the money, living with my mom and with my brother growing our weed supply. The world was my oyster.

I started reading as much as I could about dextromethorphan. I was quick to take to the abbreviation, DXM. The substance seemed to have no substantial history. Someone well versed in chemistry might disagree, but I couldn't find much. The only finding I had was that a Navy/CIA funded study for a non-addictive substitute for codeine had made the final breakthrough with the substance. Nothing more, nothing less. I instinctively didn't trust anything from the government. I decided to focus on the experiences the substance promoted instead.

There was something so ineffably real and familiar

about what I was seeing. I had had other psychedelic experiences, but there was something different about DXM. I couldn't put my finger on it, though. I always seemed to end up in the same place, sometimes for a long time, sometimes for just a moment. I wanted to call it hyperspace. It seemed like the place one would go between what I could only describe as other lives. It seemed as if I had found the Philosopher's Stone.

I was on a cloud in the abyss, with a dozen or so people on board. Fey was there. Outside of my DXM experiences, I had only ever seen Fey in my dreams. Other familiar faces would be there, but I couldn't put names to them. The dark-haired priestess-type woman from earlier was there, but I was much more absorbed with what I could see in the abyss than figuring out who she was.

I eventually had to share these experiences with my friends. Only a few of them were interested in trying DXM, and the magick was too strong the night we all did it. My friends were uncomfortable with the experience. It made me consider what a couple of months of chemical-induced strangeness could cause. Besides, it takes a long time to build a tolerance to DXM and then it takes a long time for tolerance to wear away. I figured a break would be good for me, regardless of the reason I tried to justify it. It was getting hot, too, and that felt strange with DXM.

I had gotten into a scholarship program for minority science, technology, engineering, and math majors. It began with a high school to college bridge program. The program aimed to prepare new students for the rigors of scientific study in college. We would have chances to meet and work with real scientists in a variety of fields and roles as well. I was the only physics major in the program. Only sixteen incoming freshmen were intending to study physics in a school of 20,000. I never could get over the fact that my surprise phone interview for the program came during the lingering afterglow of DXM from the night before.

I had two main takeaways from the summer bridge program, and they had very little to do with the program's goals. One was that the days of scientific research funded for the sake of discovery rather than profit were mostly gone. The other was that I wasn't quite ready to shed my innocence.

I had my first fling. I didn't think that was what was unfolding at the time, and maybe Versailles didn't think so either. I looked past her goofy name and enjoyed spending time with her. She wanted to get into social work. She was also one of the only other mixed people I had met, and the only other mixed person in our program.

There were a couple of white men in the program. The minority flag didn't apply to the majors that could participate in the Building Ohio's Sustainable Energy Future program. In a group of twelve minorities, the two white guys kind of stood out. One of them, naturally, was quite vocal about how he found it just as strange that white women were among us. Everyone else was uncomfortably aware of women's secure place among the disadvantaged.

On one of the last days of the program, Rosa, Versailles's roommate at the time, felt inclined to join us on a trip outside to smoke a bowl. Versailles didn't smoke, but she liked the smell of it. Rosa wanted to try smoking.

"I've never really done a drug I didn't have a pre-scription for," she explained.

"Well," I began.

"Yeah, no, pharmaceuticals and illegal drugs, it's *just society* and all that, we know, Nathan," Versailles said.

"Most of us just kind of had weed pegged as a stupid people thing until we met you, Nathan," Rosa clarified. I had dreadlocks and I felt like it made everyone assume I was a really into smoking weed and reggae. To be fair, they would have been half right.

We made tentative plans to smoke again when the school year started, but I didn't think much of it. I was more focused on how things would unfold with Versailles. Right up until my chance to lose my virginity arose. Then, I was overcome with thoughts of Fey. I lied and said I didn't have a condom, and things took a direction I felt more ready to deal with. It would be our last night together.

I went home for a few weeks, and then back to campus for the start of the semester. I was living with Will, a friend of a friend from my hometown who moved there just before I moved away during sophomore year of high school. When we found out we were both going to the same college with the same major and were both into psychedelic drugs, we figured we may as well be roommates. It didn't take long for DXM to factor in.

One such night, we found ourselves tragically without weed. I had never tried DXM without it and it had never occurred to me how important it was for settling my stomach after ingesting a bottle of cough medicine. To make things worse, we had spent the last of our money on getting the off-brand Robitussin in the first place. So we did what any other red-blooded American would do and turned outward to seek the answer to our problem. We started asking everyone we had met, as well as some people we hadn't met but had talked to on the internet, if they were willing to smoke with the two of us without compensation of any kind. We had no bites.

At the end of our ropes, flat broke, tripping with upset bellies, we were left with no option but to approach the resident crazy man—Robitussin Lucas, or Robo Luke for short. A few days prior, he had come to us looking for a cigarette and Will rolled him one, no questions asked. His eyes had been solid red and wide open. We figured he would, at the very least, not think us strange.

"Me too!" Luke exclaimed after we explained that we were using off-the-rack cough medicine as a means for a psychedelic experience. I was well aware of his moniker, but it was difficult to wrap my mind around being on the same page as the craziest guy in the dorm. "I don't have any weed, I got a drug test coming up, but I know a guy and I have ten bucks for you guys. I know how you feel, brothers."

"Are you sure, dude?" Will asked. This kind of

kindness didn't make any sense to either of us nor did the fact that DXM doesn't register on a drug test.

But his guy didn't answer the phone. So, we sat outside on the steps by the side entrance that people didn't use much, looked out into the dark lawn of the dorm, and talked about Jack Kerouac, DXM being the Philosopher's Stone, panpsychism, the hypersphere model of the universe, and Buddhism.

In an attempt to let go of our crippling desire for marijuana, we decided to take a walk. After nearly one entire minute of walking, we came across Rosa and her friend Blake.

"Y'all want weed? No problem. Follow me," Blake said without hesitation.

We embarked upon the trek across campus immediately thereafter. With Rosa's donation to our cause, a fat sack of weed came into our hands moments after giving up on finding any. That's how things always are, you get caught up searching and don't end up finding. But it's hard to give up the search prematurely. It doesn't count unless you're hopeless. We rolled a joint and opted to smoke it in the privacy of the cemetery of our century-old university.

"What if someone comes?" Will asked.

"I'll be able to hear them before they can hear us because of my aid," Rosa explained, casually.

"What?" Will replied.

"It's 'cause of this ear infection I've had," she said. "Until my ear recovers, I'm supposed to wear this, but I can turn the volume up and hear stuff from pretty far away. My ear should be better in like a week, though."

Comforted, we found ourselves deep in the cemetery, right outside the weathered stone door of some ancient mausoleum. Surrounded by new friends, I exhaled a deep sigh of relief along with a much-awaited cloud of weed smoke.

III

It was the day after my 19th birthday and a Friday. My neighbor had two tabs of LSD and an eighth ounce of psilocybin mushrooms for sale. Will and I, ever the scientists, did some careful research online and decided to split the two evenly. We hypothesized that if we timed the dosing just right, both would start working at the same time.

My phone rang after my first bite into my mushroom and peanut butter sandwich. It was from my mom. I had talked to her the day before, so it seemed odd that she was calling. I felt like I was tripping from the anticipation of tripping already, but decided to answer the phone. My grandpa was dead.

"What are you gonna do, man?" Will asked.

"I heard from him yesterday," I started to say and trailed off. "He sounded like he didn't really know what was going on," I trailed off again. "It seems too late to stop eating this sandwich now, so maybe it will help."

"Yeah. Well, let's walk to your car and get my camera, man."

Unsure what else to do, I stood up and we decided to walk and eat our sandwiches.

"We should eat the acid about 20 minutes after we

finish the sandwiches," I said.

"Let me smoke a cigarette before we go," Will said when we got outside.

"Look at you guys, eatin' fuckin' sandwiches and looking all happy," another neighbor, Paul, commented. He was outside smoking a cigarette. "Late for class?"

"Nah man, no classes. These are mushroom sandwiches," Will explained.

"You fuckin' guys were born in the wrong decade," Paul said after hearing the full plan. "Damn. Have a good time, guys," he said as he walked off to his class.

By the time we got to the parking lot, 20 minutes had elapsed and we ate our tabs of LSD. Inside the car, we found Will's camera and my bag of weed and paraphernalia. We had forgotten it there after a blunt cruise. Will got his camera, and we headed back to the room. We never thought about Will's camera again that night. We were preoccupied with getting some weed ready once we got back. We were about out.

Things were already getting strange. As soon as we sat down, two waves of invaders came in without knocking. First was Samantha, from my science scholarship and a sort of temporary paramour of Will's.

"My roommate's boyfriend is visiting, so I'm sexiled," she explained, "I'm crashing on your futon," she clarified. She had a huge plastic bottle of cheap vodka.

Right behind her, Iris, from my music history class entered. "Hey guys, my roommate's boyfriend is in town, so can I crash on your futon?" She was also equipped with a large plastic bottle of cheap vodka.

Iris and Samantha, who had never met, eyed each other warily. While Will was interested in Samantha and I liked Iris, both of us sincerely did not care about girls for the time being. Not even Fey. The sensations I was going through were enough to think about, even though the night had hardly begun. I could feel there was an adventure afoot, and we had to get outside to let it unfold.

Will and I exchanged glances, as we hadn't had a

moment to speak, and interrupted the girls in unison.

"We're tripping pretty hard, guys."

"Definitely gonna need to smoke some weed soon," I emphasized.

"Definitely," Will agreed. The girls didn't know how to respond. They were not pleased with anything. They didn't like that they were there together for the same reason and were quite put off by our relative disinterest in them.

"Dude! Nitrous," I exclaimed. The first time I tried nitrous oxide outside of the dentist's office was on the first night that I did DXM with Will. I literally jumped with joy that night.

"We gotta go buy some. Like, right now," Will agreed. "Need that real bad," he added, pronouncing "real" strangely to add emphasis.

"What are we supposed to do?" one of the girls asked. They didn't seem happy with how things were unfolding.

Will and I looked at each other. "I don't care," Will said, flatly.

"You guys can hang out here if you want," I added as we stepped out the door.

We closed the door in unison with Paul and his stoner-duo counterpart, JT. They were about to invite us to smoke a spliff, as was their custom. We saw each other and knew what was up—we turned to go outside without a word, just laughter. We had already forgotten about the girls and our original reason for leaving the room.

"Great minds think alike," Paul finally said when we presented our bowl at The Fence. I hadn't bothered to put it down when we left the room.

Our dorm was at the edge of campus, and there were some student apartments across the street. Between the apartments and a parking lot stood a big, white fence, shielding the apartments and the stoners who gathered around them from onlooking eyes. It was colloquially known as "The Fence."

After smoking our fill, we recalled our quest for nitrous and made for the head shop to buy some. We were regulars there, and the Iraqi immigrant and his son who ran the store were friends. Not the kind I would call up for lunch, but the kind who I would joke around with while they were working and I was buying stuff from them. His son was working.

We dropped some hints about what we were getting into.

"Have fun, guys," he said wide-eyed. "That's quite the adventure. Half of that on its own is enough," he laughed, "I've never even thought about mixing them." He tossed in a tiny pipe on the house.

The next stop was the convenience store next door for some orange juice and we could not get out of it quick enough. Our state of mind didn't seem welcome in those parts. Then, we ran into Rosa with some friends heading downtown. We moved on after greeting each other, and she later revealed that she had no idea we were tripping, she figured we were in a good mood.

Turning the corner onto the little neighborhood street that would lead us to our dorm, the troubling realization that my grandfather was dead sank in. "But I feel wonderful," I said.

"You could just be messed up or deal with it real fast, man. It's like you had to learn a new way to grieve, man," Will replied. "Do you think he'd want you moping around?"

"Yeah, you're right," I said and trailed off. "Dude, we don't have much bud left."

We approached the dorm, and one of the local drug dealers, Andy, was outside smoking a cigarette. News of our adventure was spreading, and seeing our infamous half gallons of orange juice confirmed the story. He smiled and said, "I just picked up some bud if you guys need any." We went promptly to his room, then back to ours.

It felt like hours had gone by. We had completely forgotten about Iris and Samantha, and the girls had forgotten about us. We walked in and the girls were drunk and best friends.

Without a word beyond a typical greeting, Will and I sat down and got out the nitrous paraphernalia. Our worlds briefly melted into a sea of color and sound. An indeterminate period later, and we were out of nitrous and ready for the next move. "I gotta get outside," I spat out.

"Let's go to Pride Rock!" Will said as he came out of his daze.

"Are you guys ok to be in public?" one of the girls asked.

"I've never felt better," I said, standing up. I hadn't told anyone other than Will about grandpa. I picked up my backpack and started packing for the 40-minute walk across campus to the university golf course bearing the singular hill in the county. I always liked to carry an inventory, but I rarely used anything I packed.

"When will you be back?" Iris asked.

"Literally no idea," Will said.

"Can I bum a cigarette?" Samantha asked, clearly drunk.

Will and I sat on the bench by the entrance of the dorm while Samantha and Iris stood in front of us, their drunkenness seeming like a sad, confused, sweaty haze over them.

"What are you thinking about?" Samantha asked Will.

"I'm thinking about smoking this cigarette," he said. He finished it, we said bye and left them my room key.

Turning the corner I said, "Maybe we were a little harsh on them?"

"Yeah, maybe, man. But I'm trying to ride out this trip, I can't be dealing with them drunk ladies."

"Yeah, man. I sincerely don't care about anything enough right now to deal with people," I said, and I meant it. The waters could have risen and the sky could have fallen on my back, and I still would have been smiling.

IV

Will and I crossed by a pond and watched the fog roll in while we smoked from our new pipe on our way to the golf course. The only words we shared were to confirm that we were witnessing the fog roll in and not hallucinating. We continued on our way, crossing an intersection blindly staring into the streetlight across the street, and we soon came to the Grassy Road. It was a path worn into the grass, probably from golfers, that we had discovered the first night Will did LSD.

Finally out in the flat, near featureless golf course under the stars, we came across a group of three birch trees. It was love at first sight. We each hugged a tree, and I wove some fallen leaves into my dreadlocks. We each picked up a fallen branch as a souvenir. Then we made our way to our favorite bench and looked up at the stars before heading up to Pride Rock to do the same thing. We could see the whole city from there; it was was the lone hill in the county.

What felt like months later, we were still out on the golf course and the stars were fading as the night became morning. We had been walking along the routes of the constellations we knew and the unnamed and unknown patterns we were seeing in the stars. Bright orange lights burned at ground level in the distance.

"Dude, I can't handle it. We gotta go see what the hell is over there," Will declared.

"Yeah, man. I don't think those are the lights from the city—remember when we were up the hill? We could see the city lights then and they didn't look like that," I said, confounded.

"I know, man, they can't be the city lights. They're way too close and like, orange."

We kept walking but fell back out of talking. "Dude, you gotta grow your beard out," Will picked up as he was running his hand through his own fresh, raw beard. His hair was a dirty blond, but his beard was red.

"Dude, I'm gonna try. It's already been like two weeks," I said. I couldn't really grow one.

It wasn't until we were right in front of the lights that we put together that the anomaly on the horizon was, in fact, a parking lot surrounded by common sodium-vapor lights. There wasn't a single car in the lot.

"I feel like we're in the desert," I said, taking in the sensation of warm asphalt on my bare feet. I put my sole-less suede moccasins on, but they were soaked through from the dew and I went back to carrying them.

"Yeah, this asphalt kinda sucks though. Let's hurry through to some more grass, man," Will replied. He hadn't brought his shoes in the first place.

"Yeah, we should smoke again," I said and we laughed.

I started to drag my birch branch while Will thumped the ground with his. Amid this musical magic, Will broke his branch. Disheartened, he laid it in the grass gingerly once we crossed the parking lot. It felt like it had been 40 days and 40 nights since I had felt the cool grass under my feet.

* * * * *

We got back to the dorm about twelve hours into the trip and things were still nowhere near normal. It was just before 7 am, meaning that the side entrances were still locked for the night. As we walked around the side of the dorm, Will found an abandoned fishbowl in the garbage. The RA working the overnight front desk shift was visibly amused when we came in at 6:55, barefoot, carrying a birch branch and a fishbowl with leaves in our hair, literally smiling from ear to ear. "Are you going to tell the story or what?" she asked.

We just laughed, signed our names and went to the room. There was no trace of Samantha nor Iris except the lingering scent of cheap vodka. Will had to go to marching band practice in an hour to fulfill his scholarship requirements.

Due to the size of the campus, that meant we had about 30 minutes to ourselves. We sat down and Will rolled a joint, then we adjourned to The Fence. I decided to walk with him to the music building and go watch the morning come into effect back on the golf course. I kept listening to "Plays Pretty for Baby" by Zolof the Rock and Roll Destroyer over and over, and it was getting better every time.

We parted ways and soon I found myself in one of the plastic outhouses on the golf course. Will was standing in formation with his trombone, rehearsing for the day's football game. I would later find out that we were both thinking about the same things at the same time. We both felt like we were going down the wrong path, and the most obvious reason for that, we both reasoned, was our chosen field of study.

I thought about the summer bridge program and the physicists I had met. I had wanted to do research, and they told me about the reality of getting research grants. I would not be able to get a research grant to pursue my curiosity, only to pursue money. It is difficult to get funding to research controversial things. Especially things that won't be directly and relatively quickly profitable. It occurred to me that I had been lying to myself since then about what I wanted. I was planning to spend the better part of my youth working towards something I was unlikely to be able to do. My youth would be another casualty of capitalism and greed. I was enjoying college, but that morning in the outhouse, I decided that if I was going to spend years in college, resulting in a bundle of student debt that I still didn't quite comprehend, I wanted to study something for its own sake, not for job prospects. I wanted to study the sort of thing I liked to learn about in my free time, like a foreign language or about culture. I didn't think organized society had enough life in it to last through my graduation anyway.

I stepped out of the outhouse and saw that it was beginning to rain, so I went back in and smoked a bowl away from the wind. Right there in that plastic outhouse, fourteen hours into a psychedelic experience, I decided to either dropout or change my major. I would seek out my academic adviser on Monday. At that same time, Will, marching with his trombone, decided to drop out.

I walked out of that outhouse a new man. I also saw golfers in the distance, even though it was raining. It was Saturday morning, and it was time to leave the public sphere. That period between the night and morning that no one is around, when everywhere outdoors is still a relatively private space, was over.

Walking through the parking lot in the soft rain, a car drove up and the driver asked if I wanted a ride back to the dorm. It was a campus cop car. With a head full of drugs, weed and a pipe on my person, and a run-in with the law two weeks prior, I said, "That would be great. The rain caught me a little off-guard," and I climbed into the front seat. It would be a five-minute drive, and it didn't feel right to refuse a ride when I did want one.

"So, what brings you out so early?" the cop asked.

I felt compelled to be honest. I said, "I wanted to go on a walk, and maybe climb that hill on the golf course, but it started raining."

"Yeah, it's not the best weather for a walk. It was a pretty sudden change, huh. So, what brought you to this school?" He was very friendly, and I told him my story (abridged), even the latest bit about changing my major or dropping out. The cop was the first person I talked to about that. He wished me luck. He seemed like a genuinely nice person. The other cops I had met on campus had a thing for catching Will and me with weed. They went out of their way to make sure I was being appropriately racially profiled by asking about my race every time. It was nice to meet a renegade cop who could break from the timeless tradition of institutionalized racism and the senseless war on drugs.

"Let's scare some people, huh," the cop said, smiling, and turned on his red and blue lights and sped up to the back door of the dorm. After the entire car was on the sidewalk, he slammed on the breaks. No one was around to see it.

After thanking the cop for the ride, I went to my room, took a shower and watched *Mr. Deeds* on an old VHS we had borrowed from the front desk. I was feeling great, and definitely still tripping. I closed my eyes for a bit and rested, and soon Will came in on his lunch break.

"I'm still trippin', man."

"Me too," I said, getting up to pack a bowl.

"I'm gonna drop out, dude."

"Dude, I was thinking the same thing. Or maybe I'll just change my major or something."

We smoked out at The Fence and Will went back to marching band practice for the last time. He never attended class again. My own attendance dropped and I stopped doing most of my homework, but I didn't have the same resolve as Will.

V

It was a quiet autumn day. Will and I were fresh out of cash and weed, sitting in our room watching a VHS of *Shrek* when Jimi knocked on our door for the first time.

Jimi was a goofy kid who lived down the hall from us. Will and I had smoked with him a few times with other people from our hall, but that was true for everyone in our hallway. Jimi was very interested in psychedelics and had questions for us, but we didn't really care too much about him. We didn't care about anything. One time, I saw Jimi reading manga in his room, with his name spelled on his door, not as Jimmy, but Jimi, and I thought maybe I had him all wrong. I put forth no investigative efforts, though.

"I'm on shrooms, you guys wanna hang out?" he asked when I opened the door.

"Yeah, man," I said.

"You can kinda get a contact trip from chilling with people who are tripping," Will added, sitting up from the futon, ears perked. "Do you have any more?"

"No, man, but I got some bud. Should I go get it?"

"Absolutely," Will said. Jimi stepped out of the room and Will and I shared a nod of approval.

Soon, we were at The Fence and Jimi was speaking quickly in his excitement. After a bit of relatively incoherent rambling, he summarized his story. "Yeah… Basically, I ditched my bro-y friends and took the bus across campus to go chill with you random dudes. I know you guys like to trip and those guys back there were some dumbasses," he said. He emphasized each syllable of the word "dumbasses." Will and I were gaining a reputation across campus as the two super happy dudes with jugs of orange juice. We were tripping as often as most college freshmen got drunk.

"You should do some whippets, man," Will said. Just like that, we were at the head shop reading a sign on the door, "Closed until further notice." Defeated, we stopped at a little park on the way back to the dorm to smoke more. Jimi was being very generous with his weed.

"This park is kinda creepy," I pointed out.

"Yeah, man. Yeah. Can we go?" Jimi asked.

We stopped in front of the dorm for Will to smoke a cigarette. Our neighbor/drug dealer was on his way out with a girl, and they stopped to talk.

"Oh, you're on mushrooms?" the random girl said. "I've done them like a bunch of times. They're pretty cool."

"Wow, really? You're into that sort of thing?" the neighbor asked.

Soon, they were gone. "Damn dude, I want to meet a girl like that," Will said.

"Yeah, me too."

"What? She's a liar, guys," Jimi said, sure of himself.

"How can you tell?" I asked.

"It's in her aura, dude. You didn't notice that? It's a dead give-away."

"I can't see auras, man," Will said, laughing. "Is that because you're on mushrooms?"

"What?" Jimi seemed to know that we were being honest, but was struggling to believe us. "They're easier to see on some boomers but it's not like they normally aren't there or anything." His tone made it sound like he thought this was obvious. He sounded like he was telling us what a bench is.

"Shit, man. I wish I could see auras," I said.

Back in the room, we listened to music, watched cartoons, and periodically visited The Fence, like we always did. We did the same the next day, and the day after. Our stoner duo became a stoner trio.

VI

With Jimi among us, we were becoming a proper quest-going party. One such quest became known as the Grapefruit Experience.

There is a substance in grapefruit that makes DXM stronger and last longer. We had all heard about this, but not even Robo Luke had firsthand experience. Unfortunately, Will, Rosa, Jimi, Logan and I collectively had no money for anything other than weed, nor any method of getting anymore money for a few weeks.

"If you guys can pick up everything, I can pay for everyone. I can't let a chance to dex in a big group like this go by," Robo Luke said when he heard. Despite his moniker, Luke never used the brand name of the common source of the chemical. He called it by it's chemical name or an abbreviation of it.

"Dude, really?" Logan said. He didn't know Luke as well as everyone else, and was unfamiliar with his Robin Hood-like qualities.

"Yeah, man. I've been working in the bookstore. I can get the money in a couple hours," he responded. Then he was out the door.

"I guess he can get an advance or something," Rosa said.

And so we all briefly went our separate ways to get our affairs in order for the night. Jimi, Rosa and Logan went to their rooms to do homework. Will went to buy cigarettes. I skipped my next class to take a nap.

I had a vivid dream. I was sitting at a fork in the road, waiting for something. A rock stood up, and noticed that I had seen it. The rock creature tried to hide, curling up into its normal rock shape and occasionally poking its head out, taking a few steps back until it was out of sight. I was sitting at the fork trying to understand what I had seen when I was catapulted back into waking life by a sound at the door. Will had forgotten his key and was whaling on the door, shouting for me to let him inside.

Our beds were lofted up as high as possible, with a blanket canopy stretching between the beds, sheets around the sides, and a tapestry as a door. It was an impressive and practical blanket fort. There was a lamp inside with a clapper installed, but it was rhythm activated. Sometimes speech and the TV would turn it on or off, so it seemed to do so randomly. Along with the futon and TV, it was like a different room. It gave us with some extra privacy as well as extra protection from the smoke detector so that we could smoke weed in the room. It was also an escape from our overhead florescent lights. The problem was that getting in and out of bed was a hassle. Will typically opted to sleep on the futon, while I chose to climb on my desk to get in and out of bed. Irritated by the forceful jerk from sleep, I blew off some steam by yelling that I'd be there in a second.

I let Will and Rosa in and started rolling a joint. Will soon left to use the bathroom, and I started telling Rosa about my dream.

"So… have you ever read anything about the occult?" she replied after I finished.

"Because of that dream?" I said, laughing. "I think it's interesting and I've read some stuff, but I don't really know what to think about it."

"It sounds like a dream that means something," she said

and paused. "Did I ever tell you that I'm the priestess for a little group back home? We don't really meet up anymore, but my guardian told me that I'll find another group… Anyway, it sounds like an interesting dream."

"Guardian? Like a guardian angel?"

"Yeah, but they don't have to be angels…" She stopped talking as the door opened. Will, Jimi, and Logan came in.

Will and I had met Logan when he was blackout drunk. We were talking with some of our neighbors at a picnic table in front of the dorm about robo-tripping. Logan was on his way inside, but stopped dead in his tracks when he heard the word "robo-tripping."

"You guys talking about robo? Like, DXM? You know about Zicam, right? It comes in a pink box at Meyer's. It's just like taking a shot, but of DXM. It feels way cleaner than syrup or gelcaps. Usually Zicam products don't have any DXM, but that stuff in the pink box is basically DXM dissolved into a little liquid, it's like a spray bottle. Just crack it open and drink it—it tastes awful, though," he said, and walked inside before we could respond. We saw him the next day and he had absolutely no memory of the event, but we became friends anyway.

"Do you guys want to go to a party tonight? My buddy off campus said we could come, he's cool and we could smoke inside," Logan asked as he sat down at Will's desk. Logan was lanky, blond, and thin.

"Oh, do you guys mind if Samantha comes, too? She wants to hang out so I think I'll just drink with her and you guys can trip," Rosa said. Rosa was also blond, but I always thought of her as having dark hair. She hadn't tried DXM yet, but was curious about it.

"I don't see why not," I said, carefully examining the joint I had rolled.

We ran into Luke on our way to The Fence. He gave me a handful of cash, to which Rosa asked, "Did you get an advance on your paycheck or something?"

"No, man. I just sold some textbooks from the bookstore."

Laughing, Jimi tried to clarify his meaning, "Like, you stole textbooks from your work and sold them off campus?"

"Yeah, man. I do it all the time. It's why I got the job. The place across the street will sell them at a price more students can afford."

"That's ingenious," Logan said.

Luke went back to work to finish his shift, as he had sold the textbooks while on his break. The rest of us finished our mission at The Fence and hopped on the bus to the supermarket to buy a bunch of cough suppressant and grapefruit.

Will and I had had our fair share of run-ins with the law, usually on some vague racist shit (Will was Jewish so we were a minority duo; the most dangerous kind of duo as far as the cops were concerned, so we were put at gunpoint for suspicion of smoking weed). The result of these incidents were weed tickets and suspended driver's licenses, leaving the two of us without identification to prove we were of legal age to buy cough medicine. On top of that, we hadn't planned on running into Luke and left promptly after we did, so Rosa and Logan didn't have their wallets or IDs with them either. And so Jimi was left with the task of buying seven bottles of cough medicine. Luke would need two due to his tolerance and Rosa would save hers for another night.

The supermarket only had one bottle, so we bought some grapefruit and we walked down the road to the drug store. We were likely going to need to do this anyway to get enough, but we hadn't considered that the supermarket would have so few.

"Man, you can usually only buy one at a time," I brought up, standing in front of the rack of cough medicine in the drug store. I knew from experience.

"We might have to go back and I can drive us to another store," Rosa suggested.

"Let's just give it a try," Jimi said, picking up nearly the entire inventory of generic, DXM-only cough suppressant gel caps.

"Let's wait outside," Logan said, laughing, "It'll look super sketchy if all of us are there, too, looking all baked and stuff."

We went outside, and Jimi came out less than a minute later. "Dude didn't even card me," he said smiling, carrying a white plastic bag.

We made it back to the grocery store in time to catch the bus back to campus. Rosa was going to ride it past our dorm so she could get ready for the party in her own room. "Just come to my place when you guys are ready," she said as the rest of us disembarked.

We informed Luke of our acquisition via text message. He was off work and heading towards the dorm. Logan said, "I have a psyche-up process I do before I robo that I gotta be alone for. I also like to come up alone, so I'll meet up with you guys at Rosa's dorm, too. Let's eat that grapefruit first, though."

Luke showed up and we ate the grapefruit with haste. Luke, Jimi, Will and I all followed our grapefruit with a second plateau dosage of DXM. Logan went to his room for his ritual, declining to join my ritual bowl after a dose of DXM. As the remaining four of us walked back from The Fence, Luke asked, "Can I get cigarette?"

"I'll split one with you, man," Will said. Jimi and I went into the dorm and had our first one-on-one conversation.

"Dude, have I shown you this book?" I asked, picking up an old copy of *Zen Combat* from my desk. My desk was covered in books and school supplies, with the only open space being where I had to put my feet to climb into my bed. Now there was a second area of the desk exposed.

"No, man, but I'm already hooked. What's it about?" Jimi replied.

"It starts off with this story about this dude named Moss or Mass or something wrestling a god damn bull," I replied. Jimi's jaw dropped. I continued, "The bull charges him, and he fakes falling down so he can literally grab the bull by the horns and fuckin' throws it over his shoulder. While it's down, he hits it with a classic karate chop and the bull fuckin' died right then and there."

"Holy shit."

"Dude, the butcher that paid for the bull said that there was no usable meat left."

"That's insane," Jimi said, flipping through the book's yellowed pages and diagrams of pressure points. We talked about the book for the next few minutes, but at the time, it felt like a few hours had gone by.

"I'm tripping my balls off, guys," Will said, walking in. "I have no idea how much time has gone by but I say we head to Rosa's."

"Dude, we should take the bus," Jimi said. "It's like a 45 minute walk over to her side of campus and I feel like we should have left forever ago to get there by the time Rosa is ready." Jimi was only exaggerating a little; the campus was enormous.

We stopped by Luke's room to get him, then went upstairs for Logan. Logan loaned me a real deal cape he owned for reasons that I didn't think to question. Then we went outside, across the little field and to the other wing of the dorm to buy some weed. Luke and Logan headed for Rosa's but didn't go together. Logan wanted to be alone while the drugs kicked in all the way, but we had all forgotten about that.

I had a habit of storing joint roaches—one of the smelliest objects one can hold—in the brim of my brown knit hat with ear flaps, and this night was no exception. We walked past some campus cops in the hallways, into the drug dealer's room and right back outside without any problem other than strange looks.

"We're a motley crew, man," Will said. He was wearing an old hoodie and had a bandanna around his face to keep it warm.

"We do look a bit silly," Jimi admitted. He was wearing royal purple skating shoes with no socks and a drug rug with no shirt underneath, sideburns ablaze.

I was wearing a cape.

We got on the bus right outside of the dorm, it went around the corner, stopped, and the driver got out. Jimi had a full bag of weed in his pocket. The three of us, knowing these details and with heads full of drugs kicking in in full force, shared a deep look of concern. Everyone was staring at us. "Dude, how long has it been?" I tried to whisper.

"I have no idea, man," Will said.

"I'm kinda freaking out, man," Jimi said.

Our whispers were not entirely effective, and people sitting ahead of us seemed to be smothering their laughter. "How are you guys doing?" a sinister looking, long haired, strange man asked as he moved to a closer seat.

"Fine, man," Will lied.

He and his friends were definitely laughing, intensifying our worry and paranoia. The distinctive red and blue lights of a police car flooded into the back of the bus window. Wide eyed, Jimi reached for the bag in his pocket, but the car drove past the bus. Relieved, he said, "I about had to Scooby-Doo this, dude."

"Let's get off, guys," I said.

"Where y'all headed?" the sketchy long-hair asked.

"Just to a friend's house," Will said.

"Oh, where?"

"Other side of campus…"

The stranger got the hint that we didn't want to talk and went back to his own seat. A new bus driver climbed in shortly after and we got off at the next stop to walk the rest of the way.

Stepping off the bus was like stepping into another world, but this time, a familiar and pleasant one. "That was crazy," Jimi said, visibly near speechlessness.

"We gotta smoke," Will said, urgently.

"Shit," I said, pulling the roach from my hat brim. "We must have smelled pretty strong."

"Also, dude, you're wearing Logan's fucking cape and I got this goofy bandanna on. We look like some fools," Will pointed out, again.

"And I got a drug rug on. They knew what was up," Jimi added.

Soon we were outside of Rosa's dorm and the last to have arrived. Logan led the way to the party, I followed behind with Jimi, Luke and Rosa in our wake, listening closely as I explained the ninja portion of *Zen Combat* to Jimi. Behind them were Samantha and Will. Will had lost interest in Samantha, and had explained his reasons earlier to Jimi and me in private, saying that "she just lays there." To top things off, in the depths of a DXM experience, the pleasures of the flesh are not particularly palatable. Samantha, already tipsy, was of a quite different mind. She gave up on Will, walked past Luke, tried to talk to Jimi and quickly gave up, bypassed me, and finally attached herself to the fiercely disinterested Logan.

We went to the basement as soon as we got to the party and segregated ourselves by substance in use. Samantha and Rosa sat with the hosts, who were drinking on the other side of the little room.

"Finally," Logan said. "That girl is not my type at all and is way too horny. I told her she should talk to my friend Jacob." It was Jacob's party. Other than Samantha, no one had introduced themselves to anyone. So, after a few minutes, we all exchanged pleasantries and started smoking weed together. The DXM set in even more. Luke sunk into his own world, as was his custom, Logan and Will got locked into a conversation, and Jimi and I had our own.

"This is weird," I said. "You know when you're tripping and look in the mirror, how you know it's you but just doesn't feel like it really is you?" I asked.

"Yeah, man," Jimi replied.

"I'm getting that feeling right now, dude. Like, we're the same person."

Jimi looked at me for a moment, squinted his eyes and said, "Dude. Me too. That's crazy."

Rosa had branched off from the drunk people and over-heard us. "It's like you're two sides of the same coin! It's weird, I see it, too, but at the same time, you guys don't really look alike," she added.

Will and Logan teamed up to roll a joint. This prompted the drunk people, who after their previous introductions hadn't talked to the tripping group, to introduce themselves again.

"You guys like just did this," Logan pointed out, and the tripping side of the room all nodded in agreement, even the barely-in-this-world Luke.

"It's probably been like ten minutes since you did," Jimi added with certainty.

"No, we haven't," Jacob said and all the drunk people agreed and were almost angry about it.

"You're all just tripping," someone said, writing off anything we said, making it clear that they thought we were more fucked up than they were. Which was common among drunk people who never trip. DXM gives people state-dependent memory, so while it may be hard to recall the details of the trip later, the trip itself is remembered while in the midst of it, even though sometimes it seems that things occur out of order. The whole experience of time feels jumbled. Knowing this, those of us tripping exchanged glances and let the drunken comments fade into the background.

"I think we time traveled, guys," Logan said. "It's like that Billy Pilgrim Syndrome you were talking about, Nathan. We're unstuck in time."

"I don't think time is a one-way street," I started to say, "or a street at all."

Rather than cosmic singularities, dark matter, and dark energy, the universe could be a four dimensional sphere, where time not only goes forward and backward, it goes sideways as well. There's no good analogy for a hyper-sphere—a finite, yet unbounded sphere.

* * * * *

The party eventually died down, so we left the black-lit basement and went up stairs, where we were introduced to Sir Isaac, the gravity bong. Immune to coughing, it was no problem for those of us on DXM to use any kind of weed smoking apparatus. It was love at first sight for Will and me. We were going to buy it, as the hosts of the party no longer wanted it. I took the first hit to affirm this love. Next, Will took his hit, and as he replaced the slide, it broke. Will exhaled with a laugh of both amusement and uncomfortable disappointment.

The hosts didn't mind the accident, but they wanted to get to sleep. Samantha stayed behind. And she would stay there almost every night for the rest of the school year, proving us all wrong about her intentions that night.

The rest of us began the journey back to campus. It was windy, and I was thrilled by how it made Logan's cape dance around me. I had forgotten I was wearing it.

"Being with you guys, I feel like I'm tripping, too," Rosa said. She was always feeling what other people felt. "Dude, Nathan! The way you walk reminds me so much of my friend May! I'm hearing your steps and keep expecting to see her!"

"Let's make a cult," Luke cut in after he had been silent almost the entire night. "Nathan, you gotta ask yourself: are you a shaman or a psychonaut?"

"I think I'm a shaman, man," I said without much hesitation. "This has occurred to me before, it just feels kinda right, you know?" I said. I felt like that a lot when I was tripping, like there was some clarity that my peers didn't seem to experience, like they couldn't center themselves in it or something. It made me feel like I had found the archetype I embody.

"You look like one in that cape," Rosa said. "It really suits you," she added with a pensive laugh.

Soon, we were back on campus. "I'm gonna chill up in my room, guys. Headphones, eyes closed. You know how it is," Logan said. "It was a great night. Grapefruit is a hell of a drug."

"Yeah. I'm gonna headphone it up, too," Jimi said. "My MP3 player came back to life after trying to get it to work on robo."

"I guess I should go back to my dorm," Rosa said. Will, Luke and I all volunteered to walk with her and flesh out the details of the cult.

After Rosa got to her dorm, Luke made a proposition. "To really get a cult going, we need to take this experience further. Sure, grapefruit is cool, but we should hit sigma. Plateau sigma is the type of shit you start a cult with." DXM is the dissociative hallucinogenic substance in the cough suppressant which was responsible for inducing psychedelic experiences. It is different from a lot of other drugs, though. Different doses elicit distinct effects, and playing with dosage timing produces even stranger results. We usually stuck to the second plateau. Movement, communication, and memory become fairly compromised at the higher plateaus, and we wanted to be able to walk around. Re-dosing second plateau doses could land you into a what was known as sigma. Luke had once described plateau sigma as "8 hours of schizophrenia," schizophrenia being a building block of religion.

"What's the next day like?" I asked. "Is there an afterglow?"

"You'll be pretty much out of commission, dude. It's more of a hangover than an afterglow. I gotta work tomorrow so at best I can re-dose a first plateau so I can stay up with you guys. Because it's so late in the trip, it'd be better to do third if you want to hit sigma."

"I have some stuff to do tomorrow," I said, "so I'll just do a first, too."

"I don't go to class or anything, so I'll be the guinea pig," Will said. "I think Meyer is the only place open, though. I bet we can walk it, we're already like halfway there."

It was 4 am and I was still wearing the cape. We smoked a spliff on the way to the store, which was a good hour away on foot. "Dude," I said, pointing to the ground between the road and the sidewalk, "that's a platinum credit card."

"Holy shit."

"That's some bad juju," Will said. We decided to leave it where it was and continued to walk.

When we got to the parking lot, I decided it would be a wise move to put the cape into my bag while we were in the store and undeniably within the public sphere.

"Shit. We don't have IDs," I said. "Or money."

"I have mine, but I was just gonna steal it," Luke said, flatly.

"We can pay you back," Will said. "We look sketchy enough and have weed on us, let's just buy it."

"And it seems like we should pay if we're forming a religion around the experience," I added.

It was intense inside the store. We all felt weird, like we didn't belong, and I wanted to get out as soon as possible. Without a word, we walked over to the pharmacy and picked our poison. Will and I went to wait outside to lower the coefficient of sketchiness.

Luke came out a few minutes later and handed out bottles. We each swallowed our respective doses in the parking lot with nothing to drink.

"Oops," Luke said. "I took both bottles. Work's gonna be fun." Due to his tolerance, he needed slightly over one bottle of gelcaps to hit first plateau. I only needed a half of one bottle.

"What time do you work?" asked Will.

"In like 5 hours," Luke replied. And with that, we walked back to campus as quickly as we could. The sun was rising. The credit card from before was gone.

On campus, we didn't even go inside—we went straight to The Fence and smoked a bowl. Will promptly needed to lie down, and Luke recalled that he had some things he needed to do before going to work. So, I decided to rest and meditate while Will had his experience and act as scribe in case Will had some insight.

Rosa's talk of guardians had gotten me thinking about sensing presences, like I had seen in anime, and I decided to give it a try while Will did whatever he was doing. As I sat on the floor by the door, I tried to feel every being in the room. I knew Will and I were the only people in the room, but I was convinced there were at least four beings in the room. They weren't malevolent, and one felt very familiar, like it had always been around. I thought about it and reasoned that the other had always been with Will, and that's why neither felt unfamiliar and the other two I was feeling were just Will and myself. After this discovery, I saw that a few hours had gone by and Will seemed to be asleep. So I climbed up into my bed, got out the journal I had started on the night of my first DXM experience, and wrote:

December 11, 2009

> *It begins*
> *I've entered the storm*
> *this is my life—*
> *this is our life—*
> *Tonight we open*
> *Pandora's box*
>
> *As we enter the storm alone*
> *We will leave*
> *enlightened*
> *and with everyone*
>
> *but first know that you will die*
> *just like*
> *I always knew*

And thus I took an oath of the abyss of sorts, and the line between the mundane and the mystical began to fade away.

VII

"Remember how we were talking about guardians the other day?" Rosa asked. We were alone.

"Yeah," I said from my lofted bed while she sat at Will's desk. "The other night, after we got back at the end of the night, I was trying to feel around and I think I have one, too."

"You do! That's great that you figured that out."

"How are you able to tell?"

"It's hard to explain, I can just kinda feel these things… Do you know his name?"

"I hadn't thought about it."

"Does anything come to mind?"

"… Joey? That seems silly."

"Well, that sounds like a nickname," she said, laughing. "So maybe you subconsciously know how close you two are."

"Yeah, I'd like to try to find some stuff out about that."

"Yeah… So, have you ever heard the name Raziel?"

"Sounds familiar."

"He's the archangel of mysteries."

"Oh, yeah, I think I've seen his name on Wikipedia or something. Is he your guardian?" I guessed, half-joking.

"Wow, yeah. I know it sounds crazy," she trailed off.

"It does," I laughed, "but for whatever reason, I don't really have any trouble believing you. Besides, it probably wouldn't be as easy to believe if I knew much about him," I said, climbing down from the bed to look on Wikipedia.

"I think he likes you," Rosa said. "I think he might show himself to you, and maybe Jimi. He's only showed himself to a few people I know…"

"Well, Jimi and I are basically the same person, right?"

"Oh, yeah! I forgot about that. That seems so right, though," she laughed. "That was a crazy night. I haven't seen Jimi since then, where is he?"

"I think he's in class."

"Oh, right. Did you go to class today?"

"Just one. I've been flipping a coin to decide when I go or not."

"That's interesting. You should go to your classes, but that sounds like a kind of divination," she said and paused to think.

"Check out this symbol on Raziel's Wikipedia page! I've been doodling that a lot lately." I showed her the image of a square inscribed in a triangle inscribed in a circle on the web page and in my calculus notebook.

"Whoa, that's crazy! Hey, so, I'm feeling compelled to tell you something that I don't usually tell people," she laughed nervously. "You know how we were saying you're a shaman the other day?"

I nodded as she talked, unsure what to think about where this conversation was going.

"And I told you I'm a priestess. Well, I'm something else, too… Do you know what the word apocalypse actually means?"

My interest was piqued. "It means 'unveiling,' doesn't it?"

"Yeah! Well," she seemed to be having a hard time finding the words.

"You're a horseman of the apocalypse," I guessed, again, half-joking. Her face lit up. "… and so am I?"

"Wow, yeah. You're good at this," she said, laughing.

"It's not exactly like the Bible or anything… There are a lot of mistakes in that book."

"Yeah. I used to be really interested in that, it almost seems like it's covering up some story with another one."

"Yeah! I think so, too. But the four horsemen of the unveiling… Do you know about elements? Like, not the chemical ones?" she asked, laughing a little.

"Yeah, I think my element is wind. I've read about them a little bit," I said, grinding up some weed. Will would be back from getting cigarettes soon and it would be customary to smoke some weed when he did.

"Yeah, yours is wind! That makes a lot of sense. You really were loving the wind in that cape the other night," she added, laughing. "There are five if you include spirit, which is kinda like all the elements together. Mine is spirit, but maybe with a bit more water than the others," and she stopped abruptly as a knock-knock-kick came to the door. My friends and I had established this pattern so that we wouldn't be concerned about weed being out when someone came to the door, but Rosa didn't know the drill yet. Jimi came in, and the conversation shifted.

* * * * *

A few days later, Rosa got her homework done and was ready to take the plunge into DXM. "I gotta take a break. I've been feeling real stupid lately," Will said, casually.

"Dude, I'm gonna try to hit third," Jimi said. "But I have to get some stuff done first so I'm gonna dose a bit later."

"Man, I for real don't remember anything from my third plateau or sigma or whatever," Will pointed out.

"State-dependent memory is pretty big with robo, so maybe next time you do it, you'll remember," I pointed out. "I'll do a second plateau with Rosa." I figured it would be good for her to have someone on the same page.

We went out in the light rain for the post-dosing bowl. Jimi went right back in to take his dose, putting off whatever he was going to do. We went back inside, but Rosa said she wanted to be outside again a few minutes later. I brought my notebook since it always seemed like a good thing to have during a trip. Will brought some cigarettes.

We huddled by the door to stay dry. Rosa stopped talking. With her eyes, she seemed to be saying she couldn't. I gave her my notebook. She sat down on the ground and wrote. At the top of the page, she wrote, "Rosa Pretzel is my name." She then made a list of topics.

> *The bringer of death and bringer of life will together destroy the world.*
> *The sun... heat... then gone... everything gone.*
> *That tree... So much energy.*
> *The mistress and her horsemen...*
> *Water is next!*

Will and I didn't pay much attention to what she was writing. Soon, Jimi and some of our other friends came out. The newcomers invited everyone to smoke with them in the soon-to-be-closed-campus-operated-homeless shelter. Naturally, we obliged.

"What's with her? Oh wait, she's with you guys, so she's tripping, right?" Peyton asked me as she made goofy gestures in front of Rosa. Her name was Sally, but we called her Peyton—the name she used when she was a stripper. "It was easy for guys to remember," she had explained.

Peyton was a friend of my friend Daisy's roommate. I had mentioned the fort to Daisy before and she figured she could make a better one. I met her roommate and Peyton when Will and I went to see her trash-fort.

We all went over to the shelter, which appeared to be empty, and went down to one of the rooms in the basement to smoke a blunt. There were quite a few people among us, and it felt like we were smoking for an eternity.

"Dude, this is where I got *Zen Combat* from," I told Jimi.

"Yeah, like all the books are gone now, though. This

place will be closed in like a week, dude," Peyton said.

"This room... don't stay too long... someone's coming," Rosa wrote in my notebook and showed it to me. She wasn't smoking or smiling anymore.

"Rosa, if you smoke, the trip will be smoother and we'll also be done quicker," Will pointed out. At that moment, Jimi hit the third plateau. His body fell into an odd pose— one which everyone had noticed Luke in before. "Dude, Jimi's got the T-Rex arms! We should hurry and get out of here, Jimi's not really gonna be good to go in public," Will continued, laughing.

* * * * *

Back in the room, Rosa still didn't seem to be able to speak, but wrote. "Jimi is blue, Nathan yellow, Will green... why am I so purple?" and then on the next two lines, in a somewhat different style, wrote:

Lucifer's child will come whether you want him to or not.
Time is lost but much is gained.

I was watching her write, Jimi was laying on the floor, and Will was looking for music to play. Rosa continued, still in this unusual script:

All will be well once the child is born.
The sun... and the son as one.
The eye will open and all will be seen.

With that, she had filled a page. She handed me the notebook, and I noticed she had a marked change in demeanor—she didn't have her eyes and she had this little knowing smile and her posture was impeccable. Rosa tended to slouch. Her blond hair and blue eyes seemed out of character. It always seemed like she should have black hair and dark eyes, but this was more significant than usual.

"You can write more," I said. But she just looked at me

and then to the door, smiling. There was a knock, but not a knock-knock-kick. I lifted the duct tape flap we kept over the peephole to investigate. It kept light from the room from spilling into the hallway—it was part of the system which kept people on the outside from knowing if anyone was in the room. It made us think that people wouldn't think the weed smell was coming from our room if no one seemed to be there. The neighbors were at the door, so I opened it and saw it was more than just Paul and JT. It was a big group of people who wanted to walk to the park and smoke after hearing about it from me and Will.

When nothing else was going on, Will and I had a tendency to go walking around and we had discovered the city park on one such walk. Taking a walk on the second plateau feels like you're a head floating through the environment. We called it *tumbleweedin'*.

"I don't think I can move, man," Jimi said.

Luke, who was among those insisting on going to the park, said, "Oh man, you're on third aren't you!? It feels impossible, but you can totally walk, dude."

"How could you tell?" I asked.

"Dude, he's got the T-Rex arms. It's a dead give away."

"That's why you walk around with your arms like that!" Paul said.

Luke just laughed.

"Whoa," Jimi said, standing up.

"Yeah dude, only people who've done third would even think you were tripping right now. You're pretty much unaware of your body, so moving feels super weird, but it's fun, dude," Luke explained.

Rosa maintained her unusual demeanor and remained silent. There were ten of us in total heading to the park, Will and me leading the way. "I feel like there are about 20 of us walking right now," I said looking back, surprised by the actual number.

"Dude, me too," Daves said. He lived across from Jimi and occasionally inserted himself among us. He was trying to escape his small-town, sober upbringing. "Guys, I think

I'm too big for this," he said. He had also drunk a bottle of cough medicine, but without any tutelage as to what kind to get, or how much to take. He didn't tell anyone until after he had done it, either. Daves was quite a large man, both in height and weight—he was over 300 pounds. Naturally, he was a redhead. A person of his size would need a much larger dose than someone of my size. Still, even a small bottle should have gotten him to the first plateau.

"Well, your mindset is a big thing, man. You get what you think you will with drugs like this," Luke pointed out.

"I think I'm just too big," he said, sighing.

And so the party continued. We stepped into the park and Rosa's knowing smile faded into standard happiness and confusion. "Do you guys see that?" she said, pointing to a figure in the distance.

"Whoa," Jimi articulated.

"I don't think that's a person," Luke said, cryptically.

"Yeah," I agreed. "I feel weird." There was a thin, black thing in the distance, and then it was gone. I didn't know what to make of it, and only the four of us who spoke seemed to have seen it. We walked over to a gazebo and tried to light our blunts and spliffs, but the world was against us. They wouldn't light in the wind.

"Let's just go back to The Fence." The words fell out of my mouth after what had been at least a solid five minutes of failed attempts to light something.

"This was a cool park, though," Paul said.

"I feel like there's a way more direct route here," JT said, laughing. Our path had many twists and turns—it was the only way that Will and I knew.

We stepped out of the park and a great weight was lifted from our shoulders. I could still feel the presence of all the extra people, though. It felt as if we were being followed, but the creeping sense of danger and dread vanished once we were out of the park. Once we were across the street from the park, I looked back and saw a cop car pull into the park. We faded into the neighborhood, heading towards campus.

"I think I'm going to call it a night, guys. Maybe the tussin is just making me sleepy," Daves said, not fully understanding the chemical he had ingested.

"That's not really how it works," Luke said.

"That's a good idea," Will said, eager for Daves to leave.

Rosa's silence and strange demeanor had returned, but she started to respond verbally as soon as Daves was gone. She was oddly articulate and concise. She also was showing an unusual passion for smoking weed—she normally took a hit or two, and now she was smoking like a champ. Luke's eyes widened and Rosa kept up that knowing smile.

JT, Paul, and Luke retired to their quarters after we came inside. Back to our original party, we returned to the fort. Rosa sat cross-legged in the middle of the futon, I sat to her right, Jimi to her left, and Will brought his desk chair into the fort. We were all quiet.

Will got out his camera. We hadn't thought about it since the night we got it out of my car and did acid and mushrooms. He started to film Rosa and said, "Dude, there's like a rainbow around you!"

The camera permanently died just after, before anyone else could take a look.

"It's too quiet," I pointed out after a while.

"Yes," Rosa said, turning to me. I got up and put on a record. The music sounded like European folk music of yore, but it was made by an American youth a few years prior. Legend has it that a young man dropped out of high school and traveled to Europe to absorb Balkan music and started a band, Beirut. I sat back down, and Rosa said, "You take well to suggestion, Shaman. Do you remember the Romani girl who danced to this song?" She still had that damn smile.

"I think so," I said after considering what she said for a moment.

"She was what you might call a 'gypsy.'" Rosa said and paused. "Shaman, have you not noticed?"

"I think I have."

"What the hell are you guys talking about?" Will finally said.

Rosa glared at him, "Fool." She turned to Jimi and her smile grew wider. "Seer, can you not see it?"

He nodded.

"Oh yeah, you were talking about seeing auras the other day," I mentioned.

"Yeah, I still don't get how you guys can't do that," Jimi said.

"I'm gonna take a piss and smoke a cigarette," Will said, standing up.

With Will out of the room, I felt like it was safe to ask Rosa. "Are you Raziel?"

"That is one of the names I am known to humans as, yes." Jimi and I accepted this answer without a second thought. It was like DXM had unlocked some door in Rosa's mind which gave an extra-dimensional being access to our world. Raziel assured us Rosa was fine and would return later.

Jimi and I started asking him questions. Between Raziel's cryptic answers, he always managed to find a way to insult Will, whether Will was actually around or not. Will decided to go to bed early.

I asked Raziel about past lives, if the place I had seen on my first second plateau trip was Atlantis (Rosa and I discussed Atlantis quite a bit), the history of DXM, my guardian, and things about the unveiling. Often, he would give his answer without a word.

"Are me and Jimi really the same person?" I asked.

"You know the answer to this, Shaman. You are older than the Seer, but you are the same. You, your 'soul,' as you say, is the 'child' of my Lilith and myself," he said and paused. "There are many problems with your language. It makes it difficult to discuss certain ideas… You split your soul. I am a being of light, and 'Rosa,' as you call her, is one of darkness. You wished to be a being of only darkness, and the Seer is the light which you removed. Most beings cannot do this without gravely injuring themselves. Your friend, 'Luke,' has tried this in another life and that is why his mind is the way it is. There has only been one other success in this endeavor—you know them as 'Satan' and 'Lucifer.'"

Jimi and I didn't know what to say to that.

"Shaman, as you have seen, you have lived many lives. And, as you suspect, this is your last. This is directly because of what you have done in past lives. I'm quite pleased with the form you decided to take. You've always favored chaos, and choosing to be someone like yourself is unexpected. The Seer, on the other hand," he said, turning to Jimi, "has lived far fewer lives."

"How does that work with time?" I asked.

"By human standards, the Seer lived many thousands of years as a single tree."

Jimi was delighted with this answer.

"There are rules," Raziel continued, "which even I cannot break. I can rarely tell you new information directly, you must discover most things on your own." With that, he reached for my notebook, turned the page, and wrote a series of characters upside down and mirrored. Jimi and I decided it would be best to deal with the riddle with Rosa, whenever she got back.

"Where is Rosa?" Jimi asked.

"The astral plane, as you call it. I must leave soon. Do you have more questions, Shaman?"

"What about other horsemen?" I asked after some hesitation. Rosa and I hadn't talked about it again.

"My Lilith already knows one. The two have been very close for quite some time, but she does not know herself..." He paused briefly and continued, "If you continue upon your breadcrumb trail, you will find what you seek."

"What I seek?"

Raziel just looked at me, but his face, and somehow not Rosa's face, told me it was obvious.

"The girl from my dreams?" I asked.

Raziel nodded.

I felt embarrassed. "Is Jimi a horseman?" I asked, trying to change the subject.

"You and he are the same, but he is not of the wind."

"I'm totally a water guy," Jimi added.

"Yes, he is of water. The horseman of water has passed from this earth, so Jimi may be able to fill the role."

"What about aliens?" I followed up, immediately feeling stupid.

"What do you call angels, demons, myself, anything not of this world?"

"Well, things with bodies of their own…"

"What's the difference between you and a zebra?" he asked. I smiled, embarrassed. "Are they not the same thing in a different case?"

Raziel had one last riddle for the night. "How old am I?" he asked.

"How should we know?" Jimi said and Raziel smiled.

"I am as old as humanity, as there was no 'time' before." With that, he began to meditate and soon fell back into the futon.

"Roberto?" Rosa said, looking at me.

"What? Rosa?"

"You sound strange, Roberto. Why do you jest?"

"So, my name's Nathan," I started to say. I felt compelled to ask her something. "What year is it?"

"Don't be silly, Roberto. It is 1776."

"It's 2009, dude," Jimi said. "My third is settin' in something fierce, guys, I gotta lay down," he continued as he transitioned to the floor and pulled his knit hat over his eyes.

"Why do you say these things?" Rosa said, looking very confused and troubled.

"Look," I said, pointing to the TV. It had been on mute for a long time, but I started to turn the volume up. *King of the Hill* was on.

"Please stop this strange phantasmagoria," she said, growing overwhelmed. She fell back into the futon and jolted back up. "Holy shit! Nathan? Jimi? Will?"

"Yeah. What happened?" I said, the only one of us conscious enough to respond.

"I had been in the astral plane... and I guess I went to the wrong body. It was 1776, and I was in Spain. There was a guy like you there, he looked like you, but he wasn't nice..." she said, looking at me warily.

"Was it Roberto?"

"Yes! Oh my god, how do you know that?"

"That girl was here, I guess."

"Wow. That's crazy," she trailed off. "What else happened?"

"You don't remember?"

"No... I really wasn't here. I wasn't just sleeping or something?"

"Raziel was here."

"What?" she trailed off again, unsure of how to reply.

I showed her the notebook with the riddle and tried to fill her in on all that happened. But she needed sleep, and so did I. It had been a long night. She stayed on the futon and Jimi slept sprawled out on the floor. Will was already in his bed, and I climbed up into my own. I didn't remember any hint of a dream that night.

We woke up and set to work on the riddle. Will promptly took a walk. To solve Raziel's riddle, we first wrote the letters right side up and unmirrored. The result was "ASEWPEENRLSLIAT," which we then began to unscramble. The first guess was "tis all weep Sean." "Sail Lea reap sewn" came next, and Rosa explained that her friend May was addressed as Lea by her mother.

"I've mentioned May a few times, actually," she said. "She's the one I said you walk like. Oh! She's also one of the only others who knows about Raziel." I was quite interested to hear that, but I was focused on the task at hand.

Our next guess was "reaps hew its all still a." We hadn't had one sensible answer. Then it was obvious: "All news is repeated." It was succinct and profound and open to interpretation—precisely the type of thing the King of Mysteries would leave. It was missing the "-ed," but it felt right to add it.

* * * * *

Rosa began to robo-trip at the same rate as Will, Jimi, and I (we were making a point not catch up to Luke's frequency), and like clockwork, visits from Raziel started to become quite standard. With all the weird shit developing, I was inspired to finish the school year.

Will had not attended a class in months and did not show up for his final exams. He was being kicked out for failing every class and abandoning his scholarship program. He was going to move back to his dad's house and go to trade school or something.

Logan, whose roommate had dropped out only days into the semester, was quite nervous. "I can't live with another person in these little rooms, man. Not even one of you guys," he said one day near the end of the semester.

"Shit, I hadn't thought of that," I said. "Some random dude could really fuck everything up."

"Dude, fuck it—I'll move in with you," Jimi decided. "My roommate sucks and I basically live here anyway," he reasoned. I was on board. Logan's feelings weren't hurt.

I was starting to feel like I never really stopped tripping. Everything felt so significant all the time, everything was surreal. It didn't matter if I was on drugs or not. Everything Raziel said seemed so important, so steeped in meaning, yet so fleeting and difficult to recall and comprehend. Rosa also continuously had to be updated on what had occurred. I began taking notes of the things Raziel said. Around the same time, I would occasionally be compelled to write nonsensical glyphs, like writing in an unknown language. I never understood why I felt like writing those symbols, and I still don't. We all seemed to be living in a distinctly different world than the one we started the semester in.

* * * * *

Right before winter vacation, Raziel taught me and Jimi a technique for sensing "energy" surrounding beings, both incarnate and not. He implied that it was an important and

47

practical skill for the two of us to practice.

"Think of someone you know, but not of their face. Think of the feeling of being around them. That is their energy or 'chi' as it is known to some. This is how you can sense beings around you. 'Rosa' has mentioned this to you before. It is a very useful skill... The future is not certain. There are many possible futures, and I must not tell you their details. However, this year is the last of the Fates," he said. Jimi and I were getting pretty used to him being around. Will started to leave or lay in his bed with his headphones on when Raziel made his appearances.

"Fates like in Greek mythology?" Jimi asked.

There was a knock-knock-kick at the door, and I opened it to see Luke.

His eyes widened, looking at Rosa's form, he asked "Can I get you anything?" and ran out to fetch her some water and snacks.

"Yes, the same Fates the Greeks wrote of. They will leave, and with them, many things will change. So you must be careful. Especially you," he said, looking at Jimi.

Raziel looked forward, seeing both Jimi and me sitting on his sides on the couch in the reflection of the black TV screen. "Sensing presences can help you. It can help you to know the character of strangers. Your friend knows this, and thus he recognizes me," he said as Luke came back in. Luke bowed formally and looked at me and Jimi in deep confusion after setting down some drinks and snacks.

"Do you guys know what's going on?" he said, unsure of himself.

"Yeah, man. This happens all the time," Jimi said.

"...I'll leave you to it," Luke said, leaving.

Keeping Raziel's words in mind, I started to practice sensing entities. This is how I met Suzanne. Just before the Fates left, she appeared while I was home for winter vacation. I couldn't see her, but it was as if I suddenly felt someone was in the room with me, stone-cold sober. The feeling I had from her was very similar to how Fey felt. It got me thinking that maybe Fey didn't live in a body, either. I was able to "hear" a name for her presence and texted Rosa about it.

"Whoa, so I just realized something," Rosa replied. "Remember how I said your walk reminds me of a friend from home? And that I have a friend that Raziel showed himself to? And that picture you drew right before winter break that reminded me of a friend of mine...? I don't know why I didn't think of this before... My friend, May, her guardian's name is Suzanne... and May's true name, the name of her soul... is Fae!"

VIII

It was 2010. The Fates had left, Will had left, and Jimi moved into my room. As soon as our parents left, Jimi revealed two bottles of DXM based cough suppressant gelcaps. Jimi never ended up unpacking that semester.

"That's not all, dude," he said so quickly that it sounded like one word. I could always gauge Jimi's level of excitement by the speed of his speech. "I ordered four feet of San Pedro cactus!"

"Dude! That has mescaline in it! Why four feet?"

"A dose is about one foot of cactus. I ordered it a week or so ago, so it should be here soon. I'm thinking me, you, and Luke could split it. I know mescaline is one of the only drugs he's never done."

"Dude, he dropped out, but I bet he will come to visit."

We each swallowed a bottle of gelcaps and I called Luke. He said, "I'll fuckin' walk back if I need to." As entertaining as the conversation with Luke was, it was interrupting our ritual of smoking some weed right after a DXM dosing. Otherwise, a tummy-ache was inevitable.

After getting off the phone, we rushed to The Fence, but not in time. I puked up pure red plastic and gambled that I would still trip. I did. Snow covered the vomit later that day, and it continued to snow pretty regularly and heavily for the next few months.

The cactus was delayed. Jimi had had it shipped to his house by mistake. He explained to this mother that he was going to plant them, and requested that she also mail some of the other things he forgot, namely the remote to his TV. Will took the old TV, and Jimi's was stuck on line and featured no way to get out of it without a remote. There was a built-in VCR and Logan let us borrow his Super Nintendo. That and my grandpa's record player added up to us living in some earlier age, cloistered away in our blanket fort.

The break from TV was great. Jimi's mother took her time to mail the package because she wanted to include a lot of homemade baked goods. She forgot to pack the remote. But with cactus in hand, the gods were smiling on us—our classes were canceled due to a level one snow emergency.

Rosa finally had time to come see us. She had a heavy class load and was buried in paperwork from the start of the semester. She continued her paperwork at my desk while Jimi and I set to work removing the cactus spines, skin, and other parts we didn't need to eat. Luke was on his way to campus.

Luke was not a typical person. He dropped out of school because he wanted to be a writer and figured that he needed experiences to write about rather than education. So instead of returning to his home with his father, "the sketch master," as he described him, and his poor old mother, who was horrified that Luke wasn't a Christian, he went to live with his "mistress." This woman was married to a soldier stationed in Iraq, had a child, and Luke described himself as her slave. He cooked, cleaned, and did whatever she asked of him. This arrangement started before her husband left, and he was fine with it. I never felt like asking him anything about it, but somehow came to know everything.

Luke met his mistress when he was 15 years old at a Civil War reenactment. A few years later, he dropped out of high school, ran away from home and hitchhiked from Ohio to Houston, Texas. He fell in a love with a girl, smoked crack, did all kinds of drugs with her, and when her parents found out, they kicked her out. Luke's roommates were not ok with her moving in, so Luke did the only reasonable thing and discarded his worldly possessions and moved onto the streets with her just in time for Hurricane Ivan. They'd go on crack binges and swim in floodwaters. He was having a great time, but for reasons I never heard, they broke up, he decided he wanted to become a writer, made his way back to Ohio, got in touch with who would become his mistress, and his parents paid for him to go to college until he dropped out. None of us knew how old he was.

That day, his mistress came in to drop him off as Jimi and I were taking a break from our cactus labor with some good ol' fashioned finger painting while Rosa attended to an errand. She wore pigtails, looked maybe 12 years old despite being nearly 40, and immediately loved us. After joking about staying, she finally left her slave under our questionable supervision. With Luke in our ranks, we got back to preparing the cactus for consumption, portioning it off into three little plastic tubs which had contained Jimi's mother's lovingly prepared baked goods. We soon finished, but the real task was just beginning.

Eating that cactus was grueling. It was the foulest thing I had ever eaten, and it shaped my relationship with food for years to come. Luke, who had consumed untold substances, agreed. Pure wormwood tea was like honey by comparison. I was gagging on every bite. We opened the window and set up the smoke system as the sun set so that precious, life-saving weed could settle our poor stomachs as we went through our trial. That was the night that we truly mastered our smoke system—Rosa was in the room with us and didn't realize we were smoking until she looked up from her homework and saw it.

After three hours, I had consumed one-third of my dose, while Luke and Jimi both had gotten through half of theirs.

"Guys, there's no tolerance with mescaline. Let's make this into a tea tomorrow. It'll still be gross, but more concentrated and it's just easier to drink something gross," Luke suggested.

"Oh, and if you do that, I can robo-trip while you do it!" Rosa added. Rosa didn't like tripping on school nights, even when classes were canceled during a snow emergency.

And with that, the four of us went out into the snowstorm to smoke a proper bowl. We were all tripping a little, except for Rosa, who was tripping empathetically. The snow had mostly stopped, so we took a walk while the streets were deserted. Scenes like that are one of my favorite parts about winter—public places become private, no one is around to muddle the air.

We went by the spooky park that Jimi, Will, and I had gone to on our first quest together. We had to stop, we could all sense something and it was drawing us in. Luke got out some tobacco to leave as an offering to the spirit. Rosa said she could sense the presence of a child. We entered the park.

We were in our natural formation—I was always to the right of Rosa and Jimi was to her left. Luke hadn't been accepted into the court of the Mystery King, and so he found himself walking behind us or ahead of us, not quite having an established place.

"It's asking us to follow," Rosa said. We went out through the back end of the park and turned left. The outside world was still, all the cars were being slowly buried in snow again. We got to a corner and stopped. A street light turned off, and we crossed towards it, silently accepting that we were being led. Will and I had noticed in the fall that street lights tended to act strangely around people on DXM, and the skeptical Logan had even accepted it after taking some walks with us and conducting his own experiments. There were amateur "studies" of the phenomenon online, too. But this was different; we weren't on DXM anyway. We continued, making turns based on the street lights, until eventually, Rosa stopped dead in her tracks and turned to look at the house on the right and nearly collapsed.

"This is where he lives… or lived?" she said.

"Who?" asked Jimi.

"The man who molested and killed the child."

Looking at the house, it was easy to believe. There was something sinister about it. "Is there anything we can do?" I asked, nervous.

Rosa turned around and we followed, heading towards The Fence. "No… I think the child just wanted someone to listen…. There really is evil in the world," she said, being careful to walk in the established footprints in the snow piling up on the sidewalk.

* * * * *

Back in the dorm, I finally asked about Fae and Suzanne. I had been dying to know and Rosa had been very preoccupied with her school work.

"Oh, right! I'm feeling pretty drained right now, is it ok if we talk about it more tomorrow?" she asked, as she started digging through her phone. "Here's a picture of her, though."

I saw the photo and was speechless. She was real. Not Fey, but Fae—May. The search was over.

Rosa slept on the futon, Luke on the floor, and Jimi and I on our perches atop the blanket fort. Morning came and Rosa had to go to her dorm. The rest of us had a smoke, rented some cooking pots from the front desk, and got to work making a mescaline tea in the dormitory kitchen. We would need to simmer the concoction of cactus and water for at least four hours. Longer to have a more concentrated potion, but we were far too excited to wait much longer. It felt strange to use the kitchen for so long, but there was no way we could eat any more cactus and no one else was cooking anything at the time.

"Eating that cactus makes me want to give up food," I said. None of us had eaten in over 12 hours.

"Dude, me too. Or maybe I'll only eat fruit or something," Jimi said as Luke's old silver flip-phone rang. He had a little amulet dangling from it like a Japanese schoolgirl. He left the room to answer but soon returned.

"So, there's supposed to be a really bad blizzard tonight and it's a level three snow emergency now, guys. My mistress is worried I'll be stuck here. She's gonna come to get me after she gets off work," he said, bummed.

"Shit, when is that?" I asked.

"Will you be able to drink this with us?" Jimi added.

"She'll be here about half an hour after the four-hour mark," he said with a twinkle in his eye. "Just enough time to drink it."

And so in a few hours, after taking shifts to smoke and finding out that I hadn't skipped my scholarship program meeting—it had been canceled—our potion was brewed. We poured it into three bottles, with mine having a bit more to reflect how I hadn't eaten as much cactus.

"This is still the worst thing I've ever drunk," Luke said. "I don't want to say what the flavor reminds me of."

"Come on, dude, you gotta tell us now," Jimi said.

"Well... You guys know DXM is the stuff in cough syrup, yeah? Well, it metabolizes into DXO... and comes out in your piss."

"So, you're saying this tastes worse than piss?" I wanted to confirm.

"Yeah, man," Luke said laughing. "But hopefully the trip is better."

"What's DXO like?" Jimi asked.

"It's awful, dude. Imagine DXM but without any of the euphoria or good parts," he replied and then, noticing the time, began to chug his potion.

Luke's mistress came in bearing colored pencils and markers. "You guys don't have to use your fingers now," she said, laughing and gazing at Jimi. Rosa came in soon and the mistress's demeanor changed. She didn't seem to like Luke being around other women. They soon left, and Rosa pulled out her supplies for the night.

She had enough gelcaps for a second plateau experience but then declined the advice to smoke weed promptly after. "I'll just meditate, but you guys go ahead."

So Jimi and I went off into the heaviest snow either of us had seen in our lives, a true blizzard, to go smoke a bowl at The Fence. Our old trail through the snow had drifted shut, so we silently took to clearing out a new trail to aid any other brave souls who would dare to smoke weed in a blizzard.

We returned to the room and were greeted by Raziel's knowing smile and that same Beirut record playing. "So, you probably want to smoke some weed, then?" I asked, noticing the change and having grown accustomed to Raziel and his tastes.

"Dude, let's go for a walk this time. Nobody is out and The Fence feels kinda sketchy," Jimi said.

Jimi and I enjoyed taking long walks, in any weather, and we had a standard set of adventure supplies—banana nut bread, a big bottle of water, a packed bowl, a joint, and our personal one-hit pipes and some spare weed. We kept these items on hand, ready to go at a moment's notice.

As we walked past The Fence, cops drove by. "Your senses seem to be improving, Seer," Raziel said, smiling. The snow had stopped for the time being, but emergency vehicles were still the only ones permitted on the road.

As we approached the next corner, I said, "I don't think we should go to the city park."

Raziel nodded.

"The Fence is definitely sketch," Jimi reiterated and again, Raziel nodded.

"Is there no new place?" Raziel asked. Raziel only asked questions which he knew we knew the answers to.

"Hyrule!" I exclaimed. Jimi and I had found a wide-open field and pond after a long walk along the train tracks one sunny but snowy day before the cactus arrived. We named the field Hyrule.

"Dude. We could totally hop a train," Jimi said with excitement. He had been reading a lot about Jack Kerouac.

"Yes," Raziel said.

"Dude, we got the supplies for a night or two on us now, we got these heavy coats and stuff, too. And we're kinda on the way there," I said as we turned towards Hyrule. Jimi and I both had winter coats large enough to make us look like children.

"If we go, we shall not return. Are you prepared, Shaman?"

"I wish I had my guitar," I said, thinking of Fey.

"You cannot bring anything or anyone."

"Shit. There's also Fae. I've finally found out she's really out there," I started to say.

"We do not have to go," he replied.

"What do you think, Jimi?"

"Dude, last night before we went out, I called my girlfriend back home and broke up with her, just pure mescaline insight," he said and we both laughed and Raziel's smile grew wider.

"I just can't, man," I finally said and we turned around.

So we risked a stop at The Fence. Raziel smoked the bowl in about one hit. "Raziel smokes like a champ, dude," Jimi said. "Rosa can't really smoke," he added, laughing. "I don't understand how that works." We smoked our joint and headed in. The presence of Raziel had completely normalized to us, and I stopped thinking about what that all could mean.

"What happened?" Rosa asked as we walked in. She never had any recollection of what happened when Raziel was around. We told her about it. She looked at me and said, "I'll call her tomorrow and tell her about you." Then she sat down to meditate and Jimi and I watched a silly movie. It became our favorite movie for the rest of our lives. We smoked in our room, the mescaline wore off, and I drifted off to sleep on top of the world.

IX

Rosa forgot to make the call and I was too nervous to bring it up. The next weekend, Rosa was ready to make the call, but Jimi, Logan, and I had already consumed the night's dosage of DXM. Logan didn't get assigned a roommate. One of the interesting things about taking drugs is the role of set and setting. Even stranger is that while Jimi and I were often tripping as a duo, our friendship eventually reached a point where being alone and being together was hardly any different—doing something with Jimi didn't count as doing something with anyone. We lived together and had basically the same schedule. I imagine he felt the same way, based on how we maintained our weed stock after blowing through the little jar I had brought from home. We always bought a good bit of mediocre weed that we would chain smoke out of our one-hitters and then a touch of something good that we would smoke when we were entertaining guests or when we were tripping. In the same vein, our trips were colored most by anyone other than each other. We assumed we were in for a very calm night when we toasted to Zicam with Logan, as he was easily the least odd among us.

"I thought you didn't want to trip," I said when Rosa showed up, looking bummed.

"Well, I do now. I'll go grab some. It feels like a good night to do it..."

The four of us left as soon as Rosa's DXM set in. She consented to a one-hit to tide her stomach over, and we decided to make for the city park to smoke a joint. Months earlier, Will, Rosa, and I had stumbled upon a spooky cabin there, and confronting whatever was there was sitting in the back of my mind. Something about it made my stomach turn. Will and I didn't even want to get close, neither one of us a huge fan of the heebees nor the geebees. Rosa, laughing at us, approached, got near the door, did an about-face with a long face and we all went back to the dorm. And as uncomfortable as that place had made me feel, knowing that a place which I knew nothing about could make me feel that way made me want to go back. The only thing any of us knew about this town was that it was an ancient swamp that had been drained about 100 years ago. Towns were soon built throughout it to produce productive farms, and a university was established exactly 100 years ago at the time. The school was going to make a bigger deal about for the incoming freshmen of that calendar year, though. The spattering of ancient, enormous swamp trees was also a hint of the area's swamp history.

We got lost as hell even though we had all taken the winding, twisting path that Will and I had blazed in the fall several times. Years later, I found out the most direct path from the dorm to the park was to cross the street from the dorm heading west and continue straight, but the world was a much bigger place back then.

Jimi and Logan had their headphones on, and Rosa and I walked a bit ahead and talked.

"None of this looks like we're even in the right century. Look at these houses! They're all so old, but look so new," Rosa said.

There was just something about them. I couldn't place anything in time. Bells chimed from some unseen source. There was a bright blue light ahead of us. "What the hell is that?" I said as we approached. It sounded like the entire city was in pandemonium—voices and sirens were growing louder, the wind was growing stronger, and I was getting tired and thirsty. We stopped to talk to Logan and Jimi. I turned around and the words "what the fuck" fell out my mouth when I saw the street we had traversed.

"That's so weird," Rosa added. Logan and Jimi looked back.

"What's up?" Logan said, removing his headphones.

"I swear the street just changed," Rosa said.

"It looks the same to me," Jimi said, also with his headphones off. "Dude, what the hell is going on in town?"

"Yeah, man, it's super noisy. That's so weird. You guys hear that too, right?" Logan said.

"Now that the street looks like we're in the right era, I see where we were supposed to turn," I said. The wind picked up as soon as we started walking.

Meanwhile, the DXM variety of Zicam was silently taken off the market after reports of it damaging people's sense of smell.

We entered the park and the pandemonium of the city grew louder and louder. "Dude, this is crazy. I'm getting such a weird vibe," Logan said.

"Yeah, me too," I said. We stopped walking, bracing against the wind, almost yelling to hear one another.

"What do you think we should do, Nathan?" Rosa asked, hoping I was sensing the same thing as her.

"I'm so goddamn thirsty, dude. It's too windy to smoke anyway," I said. Smoking a joint was our verbally agreed upon purpose in coming to the park in the first place. There was some other reason we were being drawn there, but I couldn't articulate what it was. I was certainly afraid of whatever it was, and the whole world seemed to be against us. So I made the executive decision to walk away.

As we hopped over the small stone fence demarcating the park onto the sidewalk, all the noise of the city, all the sirens, and the wind stopped.

"Jesus Christ," Logan said. "It was like we were being pushed out of there."

"That was crazy," Jimi added, thoughtfully.

We started to walk, and three bells from the church tolled, marking the time at 3 am, March 3rd, 2010. Rosa looked at her phone and noticed the time was, in fact, 3:03 am. "It's three bells three after three," she said.

"On three-three at that," I said.

"We missed our chance..." she started to say. "Raziel had told me about this day, and we ended up running away from our first ordeal."

X

It wasn't only whatever was at the park, though. I was running away from everything those days. What had started as flipping a coin to decide whether to go to class had grown into delegating everything off of my shoulders. Despite what I believed about psychedelic experiences bringing whatever is buried in the psyche to the surface, I wasn't interested in recognizing what the gnawing nihilism growing in me meant, and I didn't care. It had been growing for years. It had spread beyond me—I wanted to see anything that could improve the state of society, and it seemed like destruction was the only way forward. It seemed like all our ideas about what a healthy society would look like would be informed by the faulty society which we came from. Knowing that all we could build would be made of the rubble of what was left from the past, there seemed to be no way forward but to leave no rubble behind. The concept of being one of the horsemen of the apocalypse was starting to make sense. At the same time, it didn't make any sense. Then I found out about Fae. For the first time in my life, I wanted to see what sort of progress humans would be able to make. I felt like a fool, though. I had never met her, and somehow, the same breadcrumb trail that was leading me to her was beginning to seem like it would be the end of us as well. It seemed that running away was going to become a trend, but the afternoon following our trip to the park, Rosa walked into my room and thrust her phone to my ear.

"So… Rosa told me you've been dreaming about me for a long time. What are the dreams like?" she asked, with a trace of the usual skepticism in her voice.

"They're just kind of adventures, but that's pretty much all I dream about. I remember the first one with you pretty clearly."

Rosa and Jimi left the room.

"I was 14 years old. At first, I was with my cousins and we were crawling through these tubes, like the kind of tubes they have at kids play places like Chuck E Cheese or in a gerbil cage, but we were up in the air and looking down at the world below. I got to the end of a tunnel and I was in a kind of mental institution." She laughed, and I tossed in a little nervous laugh as well. "Yeah, and so I went to eat breakfast and there were these troughs of cereal," she was still laughing, "and you were there. We ate cereal and mixed different kinds together and stuff. And it's like, since then, you have pretty much always been around in my dreams, at least when I remember them."

"Wow, that's really cool… I don't usually remember my dreams," she replied.

"Meditating before you go to sleep can help," I said, quoting Raziel.

She told me about her life, and we found each other online so we could message each other directly. We started to stay in contact most of every day, all day. I consulted with Rosa and we worked out how I could visit Rosa's hometown during the upcoming spring break so that I could meet May face to face. She was interested in doing DXM with us, too. Rosa and I hoped Raziel would make an appearance. May had known about him long before I did, after all. But she wasn't very interested in that sort of thing. Raziel had warned me not to reveal anything to her

—she would find out when and if she was ready. So I held my tongue and held onto the hope that DXM would lead her to the same place as it had led me and my little group of friends.

In the meantime, the snow was finally melting and the long-awaited T-shirt Weather was fast approaching. With the snow gone, my red plastic vomit by The Fence from the first day of the semester was revealed. There's nothing quite like the sight of your own three-month-old vomit.

"I think it's time I pump the breaks on the DXM, man," I told Jimi.

"Yeah, couldn't hurt to take a tolerance break. We've been hitting it pretty hard."

We had been fortunate enough to routinely find psilocybin mushrooms throughout the winter. It didn't keep us off of DXM, though. We would mix them. We tore it up on the weekends, and the weekend started on Thursday and ended on Tuesday.

"Tearin' it up on the weekend is taking a toll on me, man. And my tolerance is getting up there."

"You gotta make a choice, dude. Follow the way of Robitussin Lucas and increase your dosage, or take like a six-month break," Jimi said. DXM tolerance builds up and down quite slowly.

* * * * *

Soon after not deciding whether to take a break or increase my dosage regimen, we found ourselves in a situation where Rosa seemed to be unable to understand English, although she could speak it. The oddest part of all is that we were drinking red wine, not red cough syrup. Rosa, who had begun to insist that Jimi and I learn about magick, had blessed the wine with the intent of it helping us understand what was actually happening around us. We hadn't learned anything, but it seemed like there had to be a reason for Raziel's visits.

With Rosa unable to understand us or read written English, but being able to speak English, I figured we should try to translate things. With Raziel's insistence of addressing me as Scribe fresh in my ear (he rarely addressed anyone by name), it occurred to me show her the symbols I had been compelled to write and various things Raziel had written. She could read them. The word "patience" was littered throughout it like a curse word.

Naturally, Jimi and I didn't know what to make of anything. But we saw what we saw, we were all experiencing the same thing. We seemed to be holding messages from an unseen source and fragments of some sacred text. We had no other explanation other than what we saw unfolding before us. All we could do was compile.

~

*All the elements coming
together as one
gathered around the center,
the knowledge;
chaos and havoc lead to
knowledge and understanding
which leads to peace
and serenity. He stands
around you as does
the other, observing, listening
and controlling. Decisions
are made, but not through
just one. All is
connected. He will
guide you, enable
and protect. Not
all things are guaranteed.
The book must not only
be read, but written; knowledge
is sacred and shared.*

~

*Confusion is a must
for translation of a sacred
text. Time reveals
all. Feathered winged, dark
and praised, unite, one*

common purpose brings them
together. Patience is virtuous
and necessary.
Patience. Patience. Patience. Patience.

~

Knowledge/experience/wisdom, not simply granted upon request.

~

All is lost, yet all will be found
upon the blank slate of existence.
The end is near the beginning.
All truths are known in time.
Doubt, fear, and worry spread as plague.
Nature will once again ensue
and peace will be found at last.
The key is within the connection of the two.
Fate no longer a factor,
all hangs as threads—
balance is all that remains,
everything fragile,
existence terminated.
Loyally profound.

~

Of course, other strange things were happening. Things started to go missing and turning up in odd places. I had lost the power cable to my guitar amp, only to find it months later knotted around the futon in Logan's room. Sometimes strange things would appear in our room, like a reed case for a clarinet. We never came up with any sort of explanation for that. Raziel figured it was faeries.

I told Jimi about my 19th birthday out on the golf course and finding those birch trees. I showed him the branch, which I still cherished.

"These trees are where one of the Fae came from. Do you know her name?" Raziel asked.

I thought for a moment and heard a name. "Rushma," I said.

Raziel's characteristic knowing smile grew wider.

"There's more than one," I added and he nodded in approval. "Akela?"

"Yes. One, Akela, you found. She was waiting for you by my request, and, as always, Shaman, you followed the Breadcrumb Trail, as you call it. But one of you was not quite as enchanted by the experience, and he is a fool." Jimi and I laughed, as Raziel's distaste for Will never ceased to amuse us. "The other, Rushma, has been sent to you by the queen of the Fae."

"...May?" I guessed.

"Why is it that you ask questions which you know the answers to? Yes, 'May.' You know that her true name is Fae."

"You dumb-dumb," Jimi added. Raziel was visually delighted by this quip.

"She is also 'dumb-dumb,' as you say. For she does not know herself, though she knows her true name." He paused. "These Fae are quite joyful creatures. Perhaps you have noticed their pranks. Not all Fae are willing to help you, as these two are." He turned to me, looked into my eyes, put his hand on my shoulder—the first time he had deliberately touched anyone—and said, abruptly, "You must be careful. Close your eyes."

I did as I was told.

"Remember, suicide is never an escape. It is the start of many, many problems, not the answer to one."

I didn't understand why he was saying that. A minute, or maybe an hour went by with Raziel's hand on my shoulder and my eyes closed as he talked to Jimi. I opened my eyes and saw that Raziel's hand was not there, but the sensation of his hand being there never left.

* * * * *

My luck was changing for the better. I had never been more excited for spring, and it was just around the corner. I had concrete plans to meet the girl from my dreams. I was actually enjoying my classes and life in general. And to top things off, I got a text from Andy The Drug Dealer that I had been waiting on all year two days before spring break.

It read, "Yo, I got some Sid. Sold a lot before I got back to campus but I saved you guys a 10 strip."

Needless to say, I dropped everything and immediately spent all my money on it, hoping that Rosa and Jimi could pay me back for their share later. As luck turned out, they could, and we all decided to take our first taste of it the following morning. "Acid is more of a daytime thing," I reasoned with Rosa, who only had experience with DXM. "On the other hand, DXM is kinda weird in the day."

Ever since eating that damn cactus, Jimi and I just ate fruit and nice bread, but Rosa, ever the mother, would occasionally bring us pizza or something more substantial. On this occasion, we convinced her that our fruit-based diet would be more suited for the day. So, Rosa came over early and breakfasted on oranges with us, as was tradition. Then we each took our selected dose of LSD. Jimi and I both ate two hits and Rosa, being rather sensitive, took one. It was Rosa and Jimi's first time with the substance.

"That's a cool painting, guys. Whose is it? Wait... is that the top of a pizza box?" Rosa asked while Jimi cut out a page of a pocket Bible he had found. I would then roll a joint with it, and Jimi would seal the Bible joint with honey, as was tradition.

"That's mine," Jimi said. "I haven't been able to sleep, so I've been painting." It was a painting of a tree, but each half of the tree showed a different world behind it.

I had noticed over the past few days that Jimi was up both later and earlier than I was.

"It reminds me of something you told me Raziel said," Rosa started to say.

"Wait, when was the last time you actually got some sleep?" I interrupted.

"In the last three days I've got maybe like an hour of sleep," Jimi replied, nonchalantly.

"Dude. That's crazy!" Rosa said as I searched for my journal with notes from Raziel.

"Literally crazy, dude. You're legally insane right now," I laughed, thumbing through the notebook. "I think you could hallucinate just from that."

"And I'm coming up on acid for the first time," Jimi laughed.

I read Raziel's words from my notebook:
Within the meadow
lies the flower you seek
The meadow, beyond the hill
Stand by the tree
and observe
you will find your way.

"Hmm… isn't Hyrule kind of a meadow?" Rosa asked.

"Yeah, kinda. There's only one hill in town though, it's not really near it or anything," Jimi said.

I read from another page:
Be on the tree
through the valley
into the Abyss
lies what you seek
find this and your
reward will be
true.

"Hmm, I don't know," Rosa said. "Well, let's go outside."

We set off for Hyrule without thinking about it. We needed to head north, to the point of leaving the road and cutting through a field. The end of the field lead to train tracks, where we walked along the tracks for most of the remainder of the journey. Rosa was vocally feeling awkward about every step of the journey, especially once we were walking on the tracks.

"We'll be able to feel a train a long time before it gets here," I said.

"And deer season is over, so we shouldn't see any hunters or anyone," Jimi added, reminding us of his hillbilly heritage.

Out of the eye of the public and with Rosa calm and reassured about our safety, I pulled out the Bible joint. Jimi found a little Bible right when we had run out of rolling papers, so it was just in time. Some of our neighbors had refused to smoke Bible pages with us, but we never thought it was disrespectful. The cops had shut down the head shop for selling nitrous without ID-ing people, and it was the only head shop we had bothered to visit. Neither of us ever felt like going somewhere else to buy papers. Plus, using honey to seal the joints added a nice subtle flavor and made the joint burn slowly. And it had us reading the Bible, right? We always made sure to pick a page that wasn't some ol' bullshit.

"How far is this place? It feels like we've been walking for hours," Rosa said, laughing.

"Dude, I have literally no idea how long it takes to get there. How long have we been walking?" Jimi asked.

"Part of that is time dilation," I said and looked at my phone. "It's been less than an hour. I swear we've been tripping for a month, though." I typed a reply to May's text message, feeling a surge of happiness from thinking about her. "I also have no idea how far away it is, but god damn it, I'm excited to meet May."

"Yeah, me too!" Rosa said.

"Remember what you told me, man. Sao-shin. Keep your heart small, nothing lasts forever," Jimi said.

"Yeah, I know, man. Keep your heart small, love with caution."

We got to Hyrule and sat down in the grass in the sun and looked up at the crisp blue sky, ate some banana nut bread, drank some water, and smoked more weed. Rosa became unable to speak but wasn't worried about it. I loaned her my pocket sketchbook from my inventory, but she didn't have much to say. None of us did. That day in the sun was one of the happiest days of my life. For the first time in a long time, no crazy shit happened, even though Jimi was legally insane from sleep deprivation and Rosa couldn't speak. The next day, we all went home for spring break.

* * * * *

Being home was actually great. I flipped a coin and ate the

acid I had been thinking about sharing with May. The trip wasn't anything special. I wanted to be alone for it, but after I took a walk, my brother showed up to see me so we played video games and smoked weed most of the trip. I don't think he knew I was tripping. Even though that disrupted my big plans to make music and meditate, I was in such a good mood that it didn't matter. A few days later, my mom dropped me off halfway between our house and Rosa's across the state.

In the car, Rosa said, "So, my parents are having a block party tonight. They're super chill and it'll be ok if we drink, too. We can walk around the block and smoke or wait until my parents go to sleep and go to the backyard. May has to work, but we'll go pick her up when she gets off."

The party started before May's shift was over. I was expecting mostly older people to be at the party, but it turned out to be a wide age range. I overheard one of my fellow youngsters say "DMT" and promptly inserted myself into the conversation.

"What's this about DMT?" I said nonchalantly.

Rosa introduced me to everyone, and then the guy responded, "I got a little bit of Dmitri left if you want it. It's not enough for me, but it would be good for a first time, maybe even for two people."

I said something along the lines of "I'll pay any amount of money for it, no questions asked."

The guy ran to his house down the street to pick it up. I was ecstatic. My nihilism prevented me from thinking I would ever grow old, so I kept my dreams small and simple. I was sure the world would end before I finished college, otherwise, I wouldn't have agreed to those student loans without a second thought. I wanted to find the girl from my dreams, lose my virginity, and also smoke DMT. It all seemed to be falling into place.

I was an excited, nervous wreck on the way to the pizza place where May worked. Worse, I needed to pee like a racehorse. I didn't ask to stop anywhere, though.

Rosa and I walked into the restaurant. May was ending her shift, coming out from the back holding a bag with her work clothes in it. Her dyed brown hair came just past her jawline, her teal eyes were radiant and I could see her pupils dilate with excitement. We had seen pictures of each other, but I would have recognized her without one. We shared a big smile and hugged. It felt more like a "long time, no see" type of situation rather than a first meeting.

"It's so nice to meet you, but it doesn't feel like the first time," I said.

"I know right? Oh, there's Rosa! Let's get going?" she said, hugging me again.

It was one of the hardest things I've ever done, but I had to pull away from her and ask where the bathroom was, as my need to urinate was surpassing everything else in my life.

Using the urinal, I felt like I had made a mistake. I probably could have held it. I had read something about how the first four minutes of meeting someone can be a microcosm of the relationship and our first interaction was cut short by something that felt like it was outside of my control. But was it, really? I felt so relieved to get the urine out of my system and I figured that bit of relationship advice didn't apply to soul mates, to souls who were together through lifetimes. I had seen her before in other lives, and Raziel had confirmed my theory. Now that I had seen her with my own eyes, I didn't think there was any way Fae could stop being in my life.

Back at Rosa's place, Rosa got a little drunk while May and I paced ourselves a bit more. Rosa went to bed early, and we were finally alone for the first time.

"This is crazy," May said. "Is this really the first time for us to meet?"

"I know, right? I want to say I've missed you."

We sat on the couch, away from the dying party, and she drifted into my arms and we drifted off to sleep together after sharing a brief kiss. The search was over, and in a way, it felt like my previous life was over. All my life goals were in reach; the game was nearly over.

I awoke to Rosa's father laughing. "You guys could have gone to the guest bedroom," he said. "You're 18, right?"

"Not 'til June, Mr. Pretzel," May said, a little embarrassed and sleepy-eyed.

After breakfast, we spent the day with Rosa and her mother running errands, May and I hand-in-hand. I had assumed it might be a challenge to get a bunch of cough medicine while staying with Rosa's parents, so I had picked up three bottles before I left home and had them securely in my bag, along with a big jar of my brother's homegrown weed that I was hoping would last me through the end of the semester.

Night fell and we each took a second plateau dose. Then the three of us took a walk to smoke some weed, but only I ended up smoking. May had smoked for the first time in her life after dinner, just a few hours ago. "I don't want to do too many new things all at once," she said. I thought it was funny how she had done LSD yet had never smoked weed.

We came inside and May went to the bathroom while Rosa and I went to her room. "I don't know, I don't think Razi will come out. I guess because Jimi isn't here," Rosa said. Her room, much like her house, did not indicate that Rosa was involved in any weird occult shit. No weird art or books of that nature were kept in sight.

"That's too bad," I said and paused. "I feel like May's been gone a long time."

"Yeah, why don't you check on her?" she suggested, closing her eyes.

I knocked on the bathroom door and there was no response. I went back to consult Rosa and she was already deep in meditation. I decided to risk seeing May doing something unsavory and went into the bathroom. I was worried that she hadn't said anything when I knocked. May was on the floor in the fetal position. "Are you ok?" I asked, kneeling by her, touching her arm.

She opened her crystalline eyes and said, "I am now. I forgot where I was and what was happening. I'm good now, though, Nathan. Thanks for finding me. Again," she laughed. "Where's Rosa?"

"She's meditating in her room. I think we should leave her alone. Where should we go?"

"We can go to the backroom," she said. Rosa's house was enormous. I could never remember what Rosa's parents did for a living, but they certainly had a comfortable home.

May dimmed the lights, I got out my computer and put on *Deja Entendu* by Brand New. We laid on the couch together and told stories to each other.

"My aunt has this farm. I think it's my favorite place in the world," she started. "It's really big and mostly just, like, pastures and woods, but we call it 'the farm.' There's a pond and a creek and my horse is out there, too."

"That sounds awesome," I replied, not knowing a more sincere way to express how I felt. She rode and trained horses and hers was even somewhat well-known. She also had a black belt in karate. I thought she was so cool. I was also hoping that her horse riding and martial arts training would help her put together that she was a horseman in the same way that I believed myself to be, but knew I couldn't bring that up to her and that that was *quite* a stretch. I told her about the faeries instead.

"Wow, that's awesome… I can't really feel those sorts of things. But it reminds me of *The Legend of Zelda*!"

"Yeah! Raziel has said that some games and stuff have some very real things in them, like the creators of things unknowingly pull bits of truth into their stories." She didn't have much to say about Raziel, but something much more pressing came up anyway. My skin was a bit darker than hers, and most of my friends for that matter, but at that moment I had literally no idea of whose arm was whose. "Is that your arm or mine?" I asked, laughing.

She laughed, "I can't tell either! That's so weird."

That moment, in the grips of one of my favorite

substances, listening to one of my favorite pieces of music at the time, losing track of whose arm was whose with the girl I had been dreaming about for the past five years was one of the best of moments I could recall. I never wanted it to end. But, like all things, that moment eventually ended, spring break ended, and Rosa and I drove back to school to finish the second half of our second half of our first year of college.

XI

Jimi and I started the remainder of the semester as if it were our last. I filled Jimi in on what I had done, and he briefly told me about his experience with the psyborg xombie—the combination of DXM and LSA, a precursor of LSD.

Luke was the one who told us about the psyborg xombie. It was on the psyborg xombie that he created the beaded artwork that he was selling on consignment at the hippy shop in town. He also got arrested that day. He told the story like this:

"So, I felt kind of normal, in a weird way. Like, my actions just seemed robotic—it was like I had mastered moving and manipulating things in such a way that I could do things without thinking about them at all. But at the same time, it was like I had no awareness, I couldn't really feel things. Like, I had my emotions, but physical sensa-tion was like, and object in my mind that I could ignore, just like thinking about an elephant or something. So, I figured, fuck it, I'll go for a drive. It was daylight and there's basically no one in my old podunk town, so I wasn't worried about other cars or anything. And I was driving fine! But then I got pulled over. So, I asked him what for, you know, I was obeying all the traffic laws and

76

everything. And he was like, 'You're naked,' and I was like, 'Oh, shit! I am naked!' So, yeah, the next few hours weren't great but jail was actually pretty fun." Luke's jail stories are another story, though.

Jimi's experience wasn't quite as spectacular—he kept his madness and nudity to himself at a campsite in the woods outside of his own podunk town.

I was more interested in what we had dubbed LSDXM—a moderate amount of LSD with a first or light second plateau dosage of DXM. Back in the winter, we had The Hemingway and The Jack Sparrow—wine with a first plateau of DXM and a second plateau of DXM with a small dose of mushrooms, respectively. They mostly lead to terse dialogue and trouble walking. LSDXM seemed like something different. Alas, I never felt the time was right for it. There was one day in the sun that we dipped into my newly acquired DMT, but it wasn't quite enough for either of us to have the "blast off" experience we had heard about. What turned out to be the most useful in our repertoire was a combination we called *brain chemicals*.

The combination known as brain chemicals was 5-HTP supplements, melatonin, and weed. The extended practice was to take one 5-HTP in the morning and then take it and melatonin at night for a few days in a row. With weed, it had this synergy that would get us really high, but also made us take better care of ourselves. 5-HTP is dangerous to mix with DXM, so we never mixed them and usually wanted a couple days in between using them. One time, Luke came to visit while were doing the extended practice. He was robo-tripping and wanted a 5-HTP. We decided to flip a coin, and it came up "no" seven times in a row. Luke said he wanted to ride into that storm, and Jimi and I told him we wouldn't lend him our boat.

After we finished telling each other about our spring break escapades, we decided the best thing we could do would be to eat some brain chemicals and each have a personal joint to see if we could get unreasonably high.

We came back inside, I dropped my roach off in my

desk and we made for the little sub shop in the basement of our dorm. The subs were terrible, but they had a fantastic drink selection and banana nut bread. Walking down, we couldn't help but notice that the group of beautiful girls ahead of us seemed to be laughing directly at Jimi. We figured they heard what we were talking about and thought he was funny. At least, that was Jimi's theory.

We were able to skip most of the line because we weren't getting sandwiches. I picked out a bottle of water and a bottle of orange juice from the glass refrigerator, and then picked out a loaf of banana nut bread from the counter. The Fox was working the cash register. Will and I started referring to her as The Fox in the fall because she never wore her name tag and was very attractive. She had worked there all year and the name stuck.

She scanned my items and I walked off to the side so Jimi could make his purchase. She turned to scan Jimi's water, and Jimi seized the opportunity to get a look at her ass. His jaw dropped, and he dropped his meal card along with it. She turned around, clearly saw what had happened, and laughed. Jimi paid and we went to check our mail.

In the mailroom, we noticed all the mailboxes were filled with bright green slips. We figured they changed the package slips from pink to green for the spring and that a lot of people had packages waiting for them after spring break. We took ours up the front desk and the same girls who were laughing at Jimi before were there renting a movie. This time, they were definitely laughing squarely at Jimi and not about anything he was saying. We had no response, and soon they left with their movie. Jimi and I stepped up to present our package slips. The guy at the desk flipped the card over, looked back at us, and then I realized that the card was an advertisement for an event. I quickly tried to explain that we had assumed it was a package slip as we hurried out of the room. Down the next corridor, we saw Paul. He immediately broke into a fit of uncontrollable laughter and informed us that we reeked of weed. Jimi had his roach in his pocket.

$$* * * * *$$

"So, it's cool if I crash with you guys this weekend?" Luke asked me on the phone one crisp spring Friday evening.

"Yeah, man. You can stay the weekend," I replied.

"Who's that?" Rosa asked. She had taken to staying in my room almost every night.

A few hours later, Luke's mistress dropped him off and gave Jimi and me some more art supplies in exchange for taking him off her hands. He had a shocking amount of luggage with him for a single weekend.

His mistress left and Luke revealed what he was packing. "Guys, I have goodies," he said as he pulled out bags of some dried plant matter, some kind of dried mushrooms, and a bag full of little origami envelopes.

"Dude, are those boomers?" Jimi asked with excitement. Despite our winter of near-weekly psilocybin mushroom experiences, we were in no way tired of them. Unfortunately, our source had dried up as soon as the weather began to warm up.

"They're amanita mushrooms, dude! Like some *Super Mario* shit."

"Oh, aren't those dissociative?" I asked.

"They're dissociative, but not like DXM. They're crazy, dude. There's an active phase and a down phase. Viking berserkers used to eat them!" Luke explained.

"Speaking of that, we should robo-trip while you're here!" Rosa said.

Luke pulled out five bottles of gel caps, "I got two for me, because of my tolerance, and one for each of you guys," he said with a smile. "Check these out, dude," he said, tossing me a big bag of some kind of dried plant matter. "They're fucking poppy pods, dude! We can make opium tea with them."

Luke was wearing his usual black tank top and camouflage pants, sweaty, sporting bloodshot, wide-open eyes.

"That's crazy, man! What's in the little envelopes?" I asked.

"Dude, this is JWH-018. It's a new synthetic cannabi-noid. All this stuff I brought is legal! Do you think people will want to buy any?" Luke said, getting out a bit of everything. "You and Jimi can get a free sample of everything for letting me crash here with my sketchy bag of drugs. Rosa, I'll give you a poppy pod for being awesome."

"Honestly, dude, we might be the only ones interested in what you're selling," Jimi said, laughing.

"Oh, let's have the poppy tea tonight. I've had lots of opiates before for medical stuff, but never for fun," Rosa said.

"Yeah! We gotta be kinda careful, though. You gotta drink the tea slowly and don't drink it more than three days in a row. Oh, dude! Is that chai? Can I have some?"

I gave him some of my chai tea and everyone brewed up some opium tea. Luke added the chai to his. The opium tea didn't taste good, so everyone other than Luke had no problem pacing ourselves. Luke's was delicious and it was gone in maybe one minute. Soon, he was essentially strung out on opium and we all had to babysit him.

Despite being pretty much locked down to keep Luke out of trouble, we still had a nice time. The next morning, it was Saturday and we sampled more of Luke's collection of legal drugs. There was a time that items seemed to disappear and reappear across the room and Jimi forgot we were tripping and figured he was crazy for a while, but otherwise, it wasn't particularly eventful. Sunday morning, with Rosa on the futon, Jimi and I perched in our beds, and Luke sprawled out on the floor, he got a phone call. Jimi and I both woke up but didn't move. We looked at each other from across the room and listened.

"Good morning, master," Luke said. "… Well… I don't think Jimi would be into that sort of thing… So, is it ok if I stay another night?"

The range of emotions that swept across Jimi's face was incredible. After so many shared psychedelic experi-ences, it was like we were perpetually on the same page.

We hadn't said a word about it, but neither of us wanted Luke to stay any longer. We also needed Rosa to go back to her dorm for a night or two so we could do our school work.

Luke went out the door and I couldn't contain myself any longer. "I wonder what she was asking about that you wouldn't be into, buddy."

"Dude. I don't want to know at all," he said, leaning over his bed to open the window. Then he packed his one-hitter with weed and topped it off with some JWH. JWH-018 was among the first synthetic weed substitutes, but Jimi and I found that it was most pleasant when mixed with actual weed. "I guess it's ok if he stays, though. I wish he would have asked us first, you know? I got some real-ass homework to do," Jimi said.

That night, Rosa did DXM while Luke got strung out on opium. Jimi and I smoked weed in our room, as was tradition, and did our homework to the best of our ability. Just before Luke fell into himself on opium, Raziel made a brief appearance, and Luke jolted up. With wide eyes, he cleaned himself up a bit and asked, "May I get you any-thing?"

Raziel just nodded. Luke went and filled a cup with water and presented it to Raziel with both hands, bowing. Jimi and I noticed this exchange but didn't comment. Raziel drank the water, Rosa came back, and Luke, in deep confusion, asked: "Are you guys aware of what the hell just happened?"

"Yeah, man. That happens all the time," Jimi said.

"Yeah, it's gotten pretty normal," I added.

"You three are the weirdest people I've ever met," Luke said, falling into his opium-induced stupor.

Monday morning, Jimi and I were thrilled to go to our morning classes. During the walk to our respective build-ings, we were able to fulfill the dream of every druggie college student—we inadvertently discussed Luke's heavy drug use within earshot of a group of prospective students and their parents.

"At least he's leaving tomorrow," Jimi said.

* * * * *

Five days later, Luke, Jimi, and I were sitting on the lawn in front of our dorm. Jimi and Luke were on DXM. Luke was likely also on other drugs on top of it. I was reading a book about Native American history for one of my classes. I still was under the impression that DXM was the Philosopher's Stone, but the last dose I had didn't quite get me where I wanted. Jimi was reading *The Electric Kool-Aid Acid Test*.

"Mind if I join you fellas?" a tall, tie-dyed man asked. "My name is Don, but people back in the Rainbow Family call me Treetop."

"Sure," I said.

Luke stopped smiling.

"Dude, you've been to the Rainbow Family Gatherings?" Jimi asked, putting his book down.

And so Don launched into stories about hippy festivals where the psychedelic drugs flowed like water and everything else that we wanted to hear. He was a hitchhiker and was waiting on his friend to come pick him up. Luke, who had been intentionally homeless and done his fair share of hitchhiking, remained silent and did not take his eyes off of Don for a moment. When Don left, Luke said, "I don't like that guy. Be careful around him, guys."

Later that day, Luke's mistress came to pick him up after his eight-day sojourn in my dorm room. Rosa went back to her room to catch up on her studies. Jimi and I finally had our room back.

"Dude, Luke is losing it," was all we had to say on the topic. "How could he not like Treetop? I hope he passes through here again sometime soon," Jimi said, and I nodded in approval.

XII

Life seemed to be going suspiciously well, but I still had a nagging uncertainty about continuing my education leftover from the first semester. I wasn't enrolled in any physics or math courses and was instead studying anthropology, Native American studies, and recording technology. Anthropology was interesting, but it wasn't a major offered at the institution. Will's insistence on never going to class or doing any school work had landed him in a tough position—people didn't want to hire a quitter. I had heard even the military had turned him away, but it was hard to believe he would want to join in the first place. Still, hearing that had me feeling committed to at least finishing the year, but nothing more was certain.

May knew all this, and in fear that I would skip classes, she told me that her mother wouldn't allow her to visit during her spring break. She was a senior in high school. Her mother and stepfather disapproved of their innocent girl dating an ambiguously ethnic guy, with dreadlocks no less.

The morning after getting this news, I went to class in a bad mood. A bad enough mood that I almost stayed back. But I liked my recording technology class and it would at least distract me for an hour, so I went. Besides, it was also what a coin flip advised.

The course was taught by a guy who was friends with the composer John Cage. I couldn't stop thinking about how weird those dudes must have been.

I got back from class and found May and Rosa talking on the futon in the fort. I was a little upset that she had lied but ecstatic to see her. It was a well-intentioned lie, so I shook it off.

"Well, it's not entirely a lie," she said. "I told my mom that Rosa was home for the weekend and she thinks I'm there. She really didn't want me to come here."

Just then, Jimi walked in with two bags of mushrooms at an eighth of an ounce apiece. After a brief discussion, we split them into four piles and soon Rosa and Jimi were on closed-eyed-headphoned adventures while May and I climbed into my bed.

"It feels so good to have you in my arms," I said.

We kissed. I looked into her eyes, blue and green and gray, and decided I'd rather not wait. "I love you," I said.

"I love you, too, Nathan," she said.

"It's crazy this is only the second time we've been around each other, I feel like I've always known you."

We kissed and talked and Rosa got up after an hour or two and insisted that May and her not stay the night.

"Come on, Rosa. I can just stay here." Her eyes took on a deeper shade of green. She had told me they would turn very green when she was angry. She was beautiful.

"Yeah, you can stay on the futon, like you usually do, Rosa."

"No, not until she's 18, Nathan."

This bothered me immensely. It's not like we would have sex with other people in the room, and I was the virgin, not May. We climbed out of my bed eventually and May borrowed my olive green hoodie and went to Rosa's dorm for the night. Jimi and I chain-smoked weed to keep my seething frustration from getting out of control. "I have my whole life to be with her, I guess missing one night isn't a big deal," I reasoned and finally allowed myself to enjoy the rest of the evening.

The following morning, Rosa and May came over early to join Jimi and me for our customary breakfast of oranges outside at a picnic table on the lawn in front of the dorm. We talked about faeries, and I told the story about the birch trees. May was still in my hoodie and her shorts weren't visible because of the size of it. With her crystal blue eyes and freckles, her little ears poking out from her short brown hair, and her bare feet on the roots of the great tree next to the picnic table, looking so happy, Rosa said, "You really are Fae," and I felt like my heart was going to explode. A moment later, May got a call from her mom and needed to leave as quickly as she came. But it was good she couldn't stay an extra night as she had planned because a storm passed through town the next day and the darkness it brought would linger.

XIII

Jimi's face lit up when he saw who was calling. Don was outside. Rosa and I waited in the room while Jimi went to let him in. "What's Raziel think of him?" I asked.

"I don't know… I feel like he might be important."

"I got goodies, friends," Don said as he worked his large self into the blanket fort. "And you must be Rosa," he said, taking her hand.

Rosa was smitten. Don presented us with his goodies—LSD coated candies. "These are pretty strong, guys. One for everyone, except the lady, she can have two." Jimi and I were a little jealous.

Luke was in town looking for an apartment. It was never entirely clear what his purpose for that was, as he didn't have a job and never elaborated on his plan. He stopped by, saw Don, and asked to speak to me outside.

"Be careful with that guy," he said. His eyes were bugged out and almost solid red.

"I think he's alright, man," I said.

Paul and JT walked up on their way back from The Fence. "Dude, who was that guy Jimi let in? He seemed sketchy as fuck," JT said. Rosa, Jimi, and Don came outside, cutting JT short. "...Take it easy, guys," he said as he went inside with Paul. Luke soon followed.

So we smoked and walked around and all the while, Don kept getting closer and closer to Rosa, slipping her more candies and whispering in her ear. Jimi seemed to be concerned, but I chalked it up to our shared jealousy of not getting more candies. Jimi wasn't smiling and was almost completely silent, and I found it weird how jealous he was. But I also didn't say anything about it.

Back in the room, Don joked about marrying Rosa, addressing her as a princess and such. "Boom! You guys are married," I joked, interrupting them. But it was getting late and I didn't want things to progress with them any further for the night. It seemed weird for them to be talking about things like that. "So, should we walk you home?" I asked. Jimi non-verbally agreed to this idea.

"No, I think I'll stay over," she said after looking at Don. Jimi clenched his jaw and glared at Don.

"Well, I'm going to lay down and listen to music, then," I said, a little irritated.

"Yeah, me too," Jimi added.

We took to our perches atop the towers of the blanket castle. The acid had run its course. I laid in bed with my headphones on wishing I had been more forceful about walking Rosa home. She wouldn't allow my girlfriend to stay over but was inviting herself to stay with a dude she had just met on my couch. But I figured the two of them wouldn't do anything with Jimi and me still in the room. After seething a bit, I fell asleep with my headphones on. It was a restless sleep.

I awoke and pale light was seeping through the window. The air was heavy. I was the last to wake and decided I wanted to go to class without flipping a coin. I wanted out of the room.

Don came in from the bathroom. "Morning, sleepy-head," he said, smiling and cheerful.

Rosa was sitting on my chair and Jimi had been standing around for the first time I could recall. Don got his bag and said, "I'm going to try to sell some furs and stuff. Wanna join?"

"No, I have class," I said. No one else said anything. As soon as Don left, Luke came to the door, as if he was waiting to check on us.

"What's up?" he said, sensing the heaviness.

"Jimi… can you tell them? …Outside?" Rosa asked, sheepishly

My heart was pounding.

Outside, Jimi said, "Well, I don't really know the best way to say this or the full story or anything… But Don raped Rosa last night."

We stood silently in the sun. The beautiful day was torture, it felt so inappropriate for the sky to be that blue.

"What do we do?" I asked, feeling helpless.

"We kill the motherfucker," Luke said, flatly.

Birds and the sounds of campus filled the gap in our conversation.

"I guess we should talk to Rosa," I said, and we went back inside.

Luke was much better at comforting her than Jimi or me. Neither of us knew what to say.

"Either I can go to the police, or we can try to do something about it ourselves," Rosa said. "A lot of people don't believe the victim… I just want a shower…"

Jimi's phone rang. "Hello? … Yes, that's me. … I only know him a little. … Yes, he stayed over, but it was only my second time meeting him. … Ok," he said and hung up. "Don got arrested for selling his stuff on campus, but they're letting him go. They wanted to make sure he wasn't lying. They want him to leave campus, though."

We waited on him to arrive to get his things. What had been a charming charisma was now becoming the mark of a sociopath. "Yeah, I've met guys like him on the road," Luke said. "It's hard to tell, but I'm always skeptical of people who seem to say just the right thing all the time."

"Yesterday on acid, I noticed he has a strange aura," Jimi added.

I felt like an idiot.

Don came into our room without knocking and told us

his story.

"Where'd you get the boots?" Jimi asked. It was the first time any of us had seen him in shoes.

"The cops gave them to me! You'd be surprised how far being friendly can get you. Cops just want people to respect them," he said. "But yeah, my friend is gonna come to pick me up soon." Getting the rest of his stuff, he leaned in and whispered something to Rosa. On his way out the door, he said, "I'll be back," and started whistling as he walked down the hallway.

Rosa started crying, looked to Jimi, Luke, and me, and said, "You can do it. The cops might not be able to get him, but I think you guys can."

With that, we discarded the furniture which Rosa said was tainted, which was most of it, took down the fort, and began living on the floor and by the sword.

XIV

Rosa didn't want to be left alone, so we made sure someone was always available. Jimi, Luke, and I planned to maintain a watch and sleep in shifts. We were going to stay sober. We all decided on this silently in the moments just after Don left.

"Luke and I are ok, but I think you guys need to go through a Rite so that you can learn to protect yourselves," she said. "He's very powerful, physically but also with magick, and you guys are basically helpless right now," she trailed off. "I think he's gotten rid of his humanity. It's like he's possessed," she paused again. "He has two elemental minions, Fire and Ice, and we need to be able to defend against them."

Jimi and I nodded. I didn't want to think about how she came about that knowledge. As for the Rite and the magick, Rosa and Raziel had mentioned things like that before. I had no strong feelings on the subject.

"In our Rite, I think we should challenge him. Let him know he hasn't won..." Rosa started to say.

"Why don't we bind one of the elementals?" Luke suggested. "I can also sling a curse at him. You guys won't take on consequences from it, only I will," he said.

The room was tense and silent. The brilliant, beautiful

day was trying to force its way into the room through the blinds.

"So, I'm going to do it whether you want me to or not," Luke continued after some thought.

Night fell. Jimi had a big metal tin that I never bothered to question, but it came in handy that night. Rosa and Luke had reasoned that we would need a container to bind a minion inside, and a metal tin seemed like the perfect vessel for such a thing.

"Nathan, do you know which way the cardinal directions are in this room?"

"Yeah, we've figured that out before," I said. "The door is north."

"Ok, you're the air element, so go to the east wall, Nathan. Jimi, you're water..." she continued, placing herself as the missing fire element. "Spirit is kind of all of them, so it will have to do for now."

Rosa read her spell and we quickly placed the lid on the tin. It seemed like a bad idea to let go, and it took an uncomfortable amount of strength to keep the lid down.

Thankfully, Raziel showed up, his knowing smile more of a scowl, advising that we step back while he held the lid down with his index finger. "Do you have something to adhere the lid to the container?" he asked.

"No, but I bet Logan has some duct tape or something," Jimi said.

"I'll go ask him," I said. I hadn't seen Logan in a while. He lent me his duct tape, no questions asked. Everyone needs duct tape now and then.

Using the tape, we sealed the tin and put it in Jimi's closet. Once it was secured and out of sight, Raziel left. Rosa began to meditate, as she did not want to take part in the next step.

"Let's sling that curse now, guys," Luke said. "Rosa doesn't need to join. Just focus on your hate and anger, everything bad, build it up into a ball, visualize it, and pass it to me. I'll do the rest. It also should help you guys feel better and let go of some of those feelings."

Jimi and I had never seen this side of Luke. He had mentioned practicing magick before, but I had no idea how thoroughly he seemed to understand it. His request to "pass" energy to him made some sense intuitively, but it was all new for me and Jimi. I imagined forming a red ball with all my negativity in it and "passed" it to Luke. Jimi did something along the same lines. Luke did what he did with it, and a sudden calm fell over the room.

Rosa opened her eyes and said, "Let's smoke some weed, guys."

We smoked at The Fence, but it didn't have the same effect as usual. At least, not for me or Jimi. In general, things were feeling different.

"That's because of the Rite," Rosa said, noticing how we weren't quite satisfied with the weed and thus packing bowl upon bowl.

"You've been officially introduced into the magickal current, so somethings are just gonna be different. But you can also manipulate that energy to make changes, that's really what magick is all about," Luke commented.

"Like, we can make superweed?" Jimi asked, sincerely. Jimi and I looked at each other with childlike excitement. Luke and Rosa both laughed.

"Yeah, you can with blessings and stuff," she said, smiling for the first time all day.

We couldn't keep smiling, though. With the challenge out, we had to be prepared for a confrontation. A true fight to the death could start at any time. Living by the sword and The Will of the Warrior stopped being jokes that Jimi and I made.

Raziel's words about energy or "chi as it is known to some humans," were beginning to sink in, and we learned to hide our energy and got better at feeling the presence of others. Jimi and I carried our pocket knives in our pockets and walked on either side of Rosa, each keeping an eye behind us or on the horizon, scanning faces.

Our dorm was no longer a safe place—it was one of the few places that Don knew. Our neighbors consented to discreetly message me or Jimi if they saw him. We weren't smiling when we made the request, and it was probably the first time any of them had ever seen us like that. Our room was already outfitted so that no one could tell if it was occupied as a part of our weed smoking system, but we still needed a place that we could let our guards down.

"There's a shop in town with hippy stuff, like gems and faery shit. Why don't we go check it out?" I suggested. I hadn't been there in months, but I remembered it fondly.

Luke had to tend to some paperwork for his new apartment, so he couldn't come. The remaining three of us arrived and saw the shop had been remodeled and now offered a wide variety of teas and organic vegetarian food.

We split a giant pot of hibiscus tea and each ordered something to eat. "Dude, this is the first time I've actually felt good eating something other than fruit ever since that cactus," Jimi said. We were on the same page.

"I haven't felt this good in a while," Rosa added. "This tea is kinda making me feel like I'm on drugs."

We spent most of the next two days there, drinking tea and talking. Seeing us let our guard down there, Rosa began to feel like we couldn't continue down the path we had chosen. Jimi and I were focused on getting more comfortable with practicing magick. The only link either of us seemed to have to our old lives was the fruit of our first magickal pursuit—the superweed. We quickly grew to understand how to use a tiny amount of weed to radically alter our sense of consciousness in several ways. Meanwhile, Luke was developing a plan for how we could capture and discreetly poison Don. In the depths of this darkness, it felt like my life had meaning for the first time.

"I can't let you guys do this. I have to go to the police," she told us one day walking back from the hippy shop.

Jimi and I silently agreed that it was obviously completely up to her. We often joked about who was the main character in our story, but we both knew it was really Rosa. We were supporting characters in her story. The first step was to drive her to the hospital. Between Luke, Jimi, and myself, none of us could come up with a valid driver's license or a car.

"You guys have done so much already. I can call Samantha. Could you guys meet us at the hospital later?"

As if she had to ask.

When Jimi, Luke, and I showed up at the hospital, a nurse approached us. "Thank you," she said. "She said you guys have kept her going," and she choked back a sob. "She was really put through hell. It's amazing that she made it through the night. She must have a strong mind. Most women would have died after being subjected to such abuse, and for so long," she choked back another sob. "And with the drugs," she trailed off. "It may be a long time until she feels better."

* * * * *

After being moved to a safe room on campus, many conversations with police officers, and emails to professors explaining our absences, the plan we had formed with Luke was altered to fit within the confines of the law. Don, being a sociopath, thought that he was smarter than everyone else. Hubris is not a virtue, but it was on our side. Perhaps he knew of our challenge but didn't think we had the strength to follow through. Rosa was not his first victim.

The cops had found that he was wanted out west as well. He was a serial rapist, a thief, a possible murderer, and a sex trafficker. They were expecting him to contact Rosa to arrange to pick her up.

"I'm coming to pick you up tomorrow," he sent in a text message while we were walking back from a meeting with the detectives. Rosa consented to be picked up from my building's parking lot, as he wanted to see his "friends."

The following night, he pulled into the parking lot at 7 o'clock sharp. He pulled into a space, a police car blocked him in, and cops materialized around his car. Don did not go into custody peacefully. The amount of drugs in his car was just below a felonious amount. The fact that he had his own car was disturbing—he had claimed to own nothing outside of the few belongings we had seen.

With Don awaiting trial, life slowly returned to normal. At least, as normal as things could be for people like us. The semester was near its end. Everything seemed to be ending. I had no desire to remain in town. The past few weeks had left a bad taste in my mouth. The previous summer seemed like a lifetime away. In one year, I had lost hope in scientific progress, had my first experiences with racial discrimination by the same two cops on three separate occasions, and felt the indirect consequences of trusting a stranger after making friends with a bunch of strangers. Everything was cast in shadow.

I would not continue my studies in that town. Jimi, a former stranger, wouldn't either. His parents were paying for his schooling under the condition that he maintained a 4.0 grade point average, and his 3.8 wouldn't cut it for them. With the city not allowing Don's presence in its jurisdiction, Rosa felt safest there and wanted to continue her studies. I couldn't understand how she could bear to remain there. But there is a chance I was projecting my frailty and cowardice onto others. The summer was upon us, and the fellowship of the Court of the Mystery King disbanded.

XV

"I don't really know what to do," I said on the phone with May. "So many things happened this last year. There were good parts about school, but I don't know."

"You seemed to enjoy it."

"Yeah. But most of what I liked didn't really have anything to do with classes. It was just nice to live with friends. I don't know if I want to find another school or what."

"You're so smart, though. I'm sure there's somewhere or something you'd like to do. You like building things! Have you ever thought about being a mechanic?" she asked.

I had never considered it. I had very little interest in cars, but I did like building things.

"My hair school has a mechanic's department, too! We could go to school together."

It was nice to have someone to talk to. It seemed like no one quite understood my situation. It was hard to explain, and it always felt like people didn't believe me when I told them about Don. I didn't tell anyone about Raziel or any of that stuff, on Raziel's advice. May was no exception to that, but I would allude to it and hope that it would lead her to a particular train of thought. But talking about my problems didn't seem to help me understand anything. Encountering evil made no sense to me. Don had used our trust against us and I couldn't understand why anyone would do what he did. Everything about Raziel both made perfect sense and absolutely no sense. And without that detail of the story, it seemed like no one saw the weight of Jimi, Rosa, and I all going our separate ways, except for maybe Luke. Everything was haunting me. Finding May was the one experience that made me feel like life was still on track. She graduated from high school about a month after I finished my first year of college.

My time spent at home waiting to go visit May was unpleasant. I love dogs and cats, but I'm allergic to them and had four waiting for me at my mom's house. Pets always made the first couple weeks home unpleasant, but I'd adjust. It seemed like my brother was making questionable decisions left and right while having a difficult time keeping his anger under control. My mom seemed to be developing a serious illness. Unable and unwilling to take responsibility for my actions, I delegated all my decisions to coin flips, whether I approved of the answer or not.

The utility of flipping a coin is in that brief moment while the coin is in the air, it becomes clear which side is desired. I chose to ignore that little voice inside; I listened to the result of the coin flip alone. A coin assured me that leaving my university was a good decision. It had told me to ask for May's advice about what to do next.

But the coin didn't seem to dictate whether to take her advice. I would ask the coin different questions related to the same issue, and got contradictory results—I would be advised not to move near her and in the next flip be advised to move to the area we were discussing living in. I was stuck in duality. We had only physically met twice, and it was driving me crazy. A coin told me to set plans with her and then later to reschedule them because of a weird vibe. I never stopped feeling like an asshole about that, and never wanted to explain how I came to that decision. Or any of my decisions. In the second week of June, a plan was made and not canceled by a coin. I made the four-hour drive across the state, got lost for two hours, and booked a hotel room with my beautiful girlfriend. There was a steakhouse near the hotel and she said it was good, so we went there on our first outing as a couple.

One of her ex-boyfriends, Patrick, seated us. She had a lot of exes and I had none. Before I had met her, Rosa told me that she had just ended a relationship and was going to try to be alone for the first time in a while. It seemed like Rosa's response to that was to introduce us.

"I have a rule not to talk to my exes, so it's kinda weird to see him here," she said.

"I can only imagine."

It was a tense meal. Whether he was or not, I felt like he was watching us the entire time. I also discovered that I no longer liked eating meat.

Back in the hotel room, she gave me one of her graduation pictures. "You really are beautiful," I said. I always felt uncomfortable complimenting people. I figured everyone knew how I felt, I didn't try to hide it.

She blushed and said, "Look at the back."

"I'll always love you, Nathan. Through dreams, you found me, and now we're just ~~four~~ six hours away," the note read. I laughed. There's nothing quite like the blinding innocence of first love. Of course, I wasn't her first love.

"I have something for you, too," I said, reaching into my bag. I pulled out a *Legend of Zelda* shirt she had seen me wear and complemented. I tossed it to her while I continued to look for her main gift. I found the little velvet box and gave her a silver amethyst ring. I felt so good, I forgot that I was also looking for my weed.

Soon, we fell into each other. I finally lost my virginity. Satisfied, it still bothered me that I went down on her, but she wasn't willing to do the same for me. It had never occurred to me that that was a possibility.

"I just don't like it, it makes me feel like a slut," she said and I decided not to press for it, but deep down I was hoping that someday she would change her mind. I didn't understand what was slutty about it, nor did I ever understand what was so bad about (a woman) being a slut.

The next thing I knew, the weekend was over and I was driving home as a new man. The drive didn't bother me at all, and I didn't get lost. All the pressure and shame of virginity I had been subconsciously dealing with was finally over. It was like I had been unaware of it until it was gone. I was glad my first time was with someone I loved. I thought it was important that it meant something.

* * * * *

The faery-tale ended when I got home.

"So, I went to the hospital," my mom started, "and I guess it's pretty serious. It's my heart."

While Raziel and coin tosses assured me that she would be fine, I still felt like everything I knew was slipping through my fingers. But May, Fae, kept me going. Hardly two weeks later I made plans to see her again, just before her birthday. Then a coin told me to delay that plan for a week because she was on her period. I never stopped feeling bad about that, either.

Things were different that time. She seemed to have something on her mind that she wouldn't say. She was always on her phone. She had grown closer to one of her guy friends over the past few weeks and had asked me if I was ok with that. I trusted that she felt the same about me as I did about her, so I didn't think it was a big deal. I assumed she was texting her friends anyway and didn't think much of it, although it was a little annoying.

Before even arriving, I had consulted a coin about bringing up the oral sex thing and ended up provoking a petty argument about it. We made up, at least verbally and somewhat physically, but I slept facing her arched back, feeling uneasy and doing my best to ignore the feeling. The next morning, before I needed to head back home, we went to sit under a mulberry tree near her old elementary school.

Still mostly looking at her phone, sitting under the mulberry tree, she said, "I wonder if Patrick can see us."

"Patrick? Is that who you've been texting?"

"Yeah, my ex. We saw him at the steakhouse last time."

"Is that the guy you asked me about hanging out with a little while back?"

"No, that was Shawn. I've never dated him. Why?"

"I'm just surprised, you said you didn't talk to your exes but you've been texting one the whole time I've been here," I stopped. "Why would he be able to see us?"

"He lives right there," she said, pointing to a house directly across from us, sounding a little annoyed.

"What? We're in front of his house? Are you trying to make him jealous or something?" I didn't know how to deal with the emotion I was feeling.

"No," was all she said.

"I can tell you're upset. What's happening?" I asked.

"I'm not upset, Nathan," she lied.

"Your eyes are green. You told me before that your eyes turn green when you're angry."

"Really, Nathan. I'm fine."

I had a hard time dismissing her fiery green eyes. I turned to Suzanne, who I could always feel quite strongly, especially around May, even though May paid her no attention. Suzanne seemed to be advising me to drop the topic. I said as much, and her eyes became a deeper shade of green.

"I don't like talking about that kind of stuff. I don't get how you and Rosa can communicate with her and I can't and you both are always saying I need to find everything for myself. Why can't you just tell me whatever that big thing is that you keep hinting about?"

We had briefly touched on this in our petty argument the night before. I told her there was a book in the hotel room, in every hotel room, inaccurate as it may be, that would have some hints as to what I was talking about in the last chapter. I thought it was a pretty big hint. She had just looked at me when I said that, and the petty argument went back to me not understanding her sexual preferences.

Raziel had said that Fae's identity as a fellow horseman

was not something anyone could tell her directly. If she was willing to accept that calling, she would have to figure it out on her own, like as Rosa and I had. "It's Raziel," I tried to explain, "We can only give you hints. I get all tongue-tied when I try to do anything more." I tried to continue but was tongue-tied. "Right now is a prime example," I finally said with a nervous laugh.

She stared at me with her beautiful, burning green eyes.

"You don't seem to want to take the hints, anyway."

"I don't want that kind of life, Nathan," she said. "It's too strange."

We finally moved onto a more pleasant topic, Japan. I had to leave in about an hour to get home before it was too dark out. I briefly met her mother before parting ways, and she was nowhere near the hate-filled racist that May had described before.

"She wouldn't be like that your face," she explained. "Besides, it's really more my stepdad that's bad, and she kinda follows his lead."

Soon, I was on the road home, not feeling as good as I had last time. I had burned a CD for that trip and to give to May, but she said it was boring so I ended up not offering it to her. "Next time," I said to myself, "it'll be better."

XVI

"I don't want to argue with you anymore," May said in a text. Following a coin's advice, I had provoked another petty argument. It was still bothering me. I knew it was stupid to bring it up again, a bad time to do so since she needed to go to work, and a conversation best had in person or at least on the phone, if at all. But I didn't listen to my intuition, I flipped coins instead.

I smoked a bowl, felt awful, and apologized soon after. I sat looking at my phone until her shift ended, and then I tried to call. She didn't pick up. A deep fear rose in me that something had happened to her and the last she had heard from me had been petty, hurtful, and selfish. I couldn't get much sleep that night.

In the morning, I got on the Internet and the first thing on my social network's news feed read "May is now single." It already had ten "likes" and comments saying things like "good riddance."

In despair and anger, I went back to messaging her from that site, where we had first found each other while talking on Rosa's phone. Among other things, I wrote, "You don't even resemble Fae anymore." I was convinced that she wasn't acting like herself and that she was aware of the gravity of everything that Rosa and I had been hinting at and was running away from it and everything related to it, including her destiny and identity. Years later, it would become clear that she just wasn't living up to the ideal of her I had built in my dreams over the years, and somehow, I thought that was her fault.

She finally replied. "I don't even know anything about you! I have no idea what is happening with you, Rosa, Jimi, and Raziel and all that stuff. You keep wanting to pull me into it but I'm clearly not ready for whatever it is and you won't just accept that. And I can't even talk about you at home, with my own mother! And I don't want to 'return the favor,' and I shouldn't need to explain why. I know what I like. Maybe you'd be better off with another virgin."

In a way, this was the most direct either of us had been with each other, and I was surprised she felt that way. I tried my best not to respond in anger anymore, I felt bad about what I had already said and didn't want to hurt her. But I was hurt and desperate to hold on to her. I tried to apologize.

"I just need some time, Nathan."

So, I waited. "Couples have fights, and this is our first big one," I thought. "We'll work things out."

In my misery, it came up that my family and friends, for the most part, didn't buy the dream story, and so no one seemed to understand what I was going through. It wasn't a typical heartbreak for me. It wasn't a four-month relationship ending; she was a girl I had known in dreams for years. Once I had found her, I never considered that things might not work out. People advised me to find another girlfriend, yet failed to illustrate how to go about that. I had always been looking for a specific person, not just someone.

"I get why Raziel had that suicide talk with me now. This is awful," I wrote to Rosa. "I can hardly bring myself to play my Fey guitar." I had been writing a song for Fae.

"Yeah... It's tough. I kinda agree with both of you about different things. There's maybe some things she should have told you earlier and some things you probably shouldn't have said. I think you guys will work it out, though," Rosa replied.

A week passed. Ten days after my last bit of bad news on a social networking site, I saw that May had a new boyfriend. This time it was the friend she had asked me about seeing before.

"I thought we were just taking a break... How could you move on so quickly?" I finally texted her after it was clear she was not willing to speak to me on the phone.

"I don't know what to say," was her reply and the last thing I ever heard from her.

XVII

"Now, they think it's cancer," my mother said. "They won't know until after the surgery… It will be a risky operation."

I still believed Raziel when he said things would work out, so I tried to be optimistic. But I had to get out of the house, I needed out of my world. I had moved to that town in high school and essentially had one friend there who I still liked, Kelsie.

"Dude, you should come over," she said. We had hung out a few times, and I always thought she was interesting and particularly beautiful. I kept that to myself, though. Strange things always seemed to happen around her. Every time we hung out, I went home inspired to write music.

I went over to her house, and since her father wasn't home, we sat out on the back porch and smoked weed together.

"Look at the moon," I said, shocked.

"Are those clouds? …No. What the hell?" she was equally confused.

I looked back to the Earth and noticed she had a new tattoo—it was a skeleton key behind her ear. "God damn it, she is awesome," I thought. Something seemed to be passing over the full moon, and the sky was momentarily black.

"I think we've only ever hung out on full moons, dude,"

she pointed out.

The thought of a lunar eclipse came up, but this change was much too sudden.

The moon came back and we went inside and watched *The Dark Crystal*. "It feels so good to be out of the house and around someone else," I blurted out.

"Dude, you have such a crazy story, I'm glad to hear it." It felt good for someone to believe me, for someone to listen and not try to fix everything. My brother and mother kept urging me to find a new girlfriend, but Kelsie encouraged me to be with friends and acknowledged that it might take a while for me to feel better. I had actually always liked her, but, like all other girls who weren't Fae, I didn't try to pursue her when I was in high school. I had been holding out for Fae.

"Sometimes, you've got to embrace chaos," she told me.

"It's too soon now," I thought, "but maybe in a while, I'll tell her." Driving home, I felt a bit more like my old self. I ran over a opossum during the drive and that brought me down a notch. I had never killed something like that and it made me feel terrible for a while. But it was a different terrible than I had been feeling, and in a way, was like a breath of fresh air.

I got home and was not afraid to go to sleep for the first time since May had left me a month earlier. Every night, I'd see May in my dreams, as I had for years, remember what happened, and wake up. But that night, for the first time since middle school, I did not dream of Fae.

XVIII

A week later, I needed out of the house again. My broken heart and sick mom were too much to deal with at the same time. The plan was to do mushrooms with one of my oldest friends in the world, Ted. Another friend would join us, Henry, which was fine. The plan to bond over mushrooms and music collapsed when I arrived at Ted's parent's house in my hometown and found myself being introduced to some new people.

Ted and I had been good friends since elementary school. I had also shared some great times with Henry. Will had brought him up to visit once during the winter and he did the Jack Sparrow while Jimi and I had DXM (Jimi's first first plateau) and Will just had weed. The day after, we went to see Ted at his little liberal arts school. Will got alcohol poisoning and his dad had to come from across the state to get him. When Henry dropped Jimi and me off at our school, he remarked how "not everyone makes it back from a real journey."

Ted's drug experience was limited to weed and alcohol, so Henry and I devised a first trip for him. We had planned to hang out at Ted's house and make music together and sit around a fire—the only thing different from normal is that we'd be on mushrooms instead of smoking weed.

Phil and Nick had been in a band with Ted, so he invited them for the musical potential. Phil had experimented with psychedelic drugs in the past, but Nick hadn't nor had he done any research on the topic, so he seemed to base his ideas on what to expect from TV and movies.

"We should go to the woods!" Nick suggested. On the surface, it wasn't a bad idea. We ate our mushrooms and Henry drove everyone to the woods before the effects set in.

Sitting in the front seat, I asked, "How are we gonna get back?"

"I can drive but I wouldn't feel right driving everyone, especially those kids," Henry said. It always surprised me how deep voice his voice was. He was a year older than Ted and me and nearly three years older than Phil and Nick. They still had another year left of high school while Henry had finished two years in the military.

"Yeah, maybe we can walk," I said.

"If it was just you and Ted I'd be good, but yeah," he said as we pulled into a large wooded park, "I'm starting to think that driving here at sundown to go to the woods with a bunch of inexperienced people might have been a bad idea," he continued, laughing.

Everyone had had the same idea to roll a joint before coming to meet each other. Rather than rationing them out, we chose to each smoke our own. But not just anywhere. "Let's go to the Tiki God," Ted suggested. The forest was colloquially known as the Hundred Acre Woods, and it was host to several named spots. The Tiki God was a spot near some trees where someone had put a Tiki head.

"I don't know how to get there in the dark," Henry said. "You're the boy scout."

And so we followed Ted into the woods as darkness consumed it. About 15 minutes later, when the mushrooms were starting to kick in and a smoke would have been ideal, Henry called out, "Are we almost there?"

"Where?" Ted, the leader of the group, responded.

Nick had been incessantly talking to Phil about his

unusual-outside-of-television experience while Phil grew less and less responsive. No one else had been doing much talking.

"To the Tiki God, man," Henry replied, sounding confused.

"I thought we were trying to get out of the woods," Ted said, concerned. "I have no idea where we are."

We had taken a lot of twists and turns, so turning back after Henry and I convinced Ted that this was the best way out, was not an easy task. Our side of the earth had turned away from the sun completely.

After an immeasurable time spent blindly wandering through the woods, we finally emerged in someone's back-yard. The lights were off, but we whispered, acting as if it were deep into the night and not just past 9 pm.

"We gotta run for it," Ted said.

"I'm pretty sure no one is home, man," Henry replied.

"And it's sketchier if we run out like we've been up to no good instead of just lost in the woods," I added.

"But we *have* been up to no good," Nick said. Nick was bothering me.

"And we got a ton of weed on us," Ted said, still concerned.

"Dude, it's dark and they don't have any lights on. No one is home. If there's anybody on the other side of the house, it'll be mad sketchy if they see us running out," Henry explained, calmly.

And with that, Ted, Phil, and Nick took off running through the yard. Henry and I shared a heavy sigh and started walking. We found the three standing in the middle of the street, looking confused and relieved to see us.

"What took you guys so long?" Ted asked.

"Dude, we walked," Henry replied.

"We were waiting here for like half an hour," Nick said.

Henry and I laughed, "That's the mushrooms, guys. Time gets weird," I said. "Let's get out of the street."

Henry and I shepherded the group to a tree in front of an empty lot and tried to get our bearings. "We're like a block away from my car," Henry said, seeing the main street off to the right of us. "I don't think those guys should walk it and I definitely shouldn't drive everyone."

"Yeah, I'll call Larry," I said. "I'm not really tripping," I added.

"Yeah, me neither. I still feel weird about driving myself, though."

On the phone, Larry, another childhood friend of mine, said he had just got off work and could pick us up and take us to Ted's. It would be about ten minutes. Henry assumed that his car was about a ten-minute walk away, so he left me in charge and we decided to meet up at Ted's.

Not a single minute had I been off the phone did Ted say, "Larry forgot, dude. Let's just walk."

"It's seriously been one minute, dude, he's on the way," I said, showing Ted the time and the call history on my phone.

Ted had to be sure, so he called Larry. Larry reassured him that he was on the way. Ted did this about three times. After about ten minutes, Larry showed up. Nick and Phil laid in the back of his truck while Ted and I got in the front.

"Thanks, man," I said, sitting in the middle.

"No problem, I just got off work."

"We got some weed you can partake with us, buddy," I added.

"Dude, we always sit in this formation," Ted noticed. He was right. I was always in the middle with Ted to my right and Larry to my left. We laughed and Larry turned on some good ol' classic rock.

"Dude, my car was maybe a one minute walk away," Henry said, smiling and leaning his lanky self against his car as we pulled up.

"How was the drive?" I asked.

"Not too bad. I've driven enough that it's like wired into my brain."

"The Beatles," Phil cut in.

"Yeah, we listened to the Beatles in the car," Larry

said.

"What time is it?" Phil asked. Someone told him, to which he replied, "Something good is happening."

We laughed and agreed and went around to Ted's backyard to the fire pit. We had prepared it earlier, so all that was left to do was light it. Ted The Boy Scout did the honors, and everyone sat and stared into the blaze in silence.

"The Beatles," Phil said, breaking the silence after a few minutes.

"We should play some music," Henry suggested.

"I can't," Ted said, looking nervous.

"I can play for you guys," Larry suggested.

"Oh, yeah, we can smoke a joint if you serenade us," Henry added. Larry ran inside and got one of the acoustic guitars.

"What time is it?" Phil asked.

"I think that kid is stuck in a loop," Henry said.

"Something good is happening," Phil replied.

Nick then went on to describe the cartoon-like visions he was having. Henry and I shared a sigh.

"You doing alright?" I asked Ted, trying to pass him the joint.

"I don't know, man. I feel like my parents are gonna freak."

"Dude, your parents are some of the most chill people I have met in my entire life," Henry said. "If they somehow found out we were tripping, they'd probably just joke with us and your dad would play music for us. Now hit that joint and pass it, dude. It will make you feel better."

"If you're feeling uncomfortable, try putting your bare feet on the ground," I suggested. "It's grounding. You could also drink some milk." I got up and passed the joint to Henry, as Ted wouldn't touch it.

Despite feeling pretty good and being almost sober, Henry and I both took our shoes off and put our feet in the grass.

"My feet will get all dirty," Ted said. It was the first

time in his life that he declined doing something because it would get him dirty. Henry, Larry, and I all knew this and did not know how to respond.

Phil went through his loop and Nick made some stupid comments. Ted continued to not take anyone's advice and grew more and more uncomfortable. Larry kept playing the guitar.

"You guys are welcome to stay," Ted said, abruptly, "but I gotta go lay down." And without another word, such as where we could find a blanket or where specifically we could stay, he went into his house.

"Well, fuck. I think I'm gonna go home," Henry said. "My house is around the corner."

"I can make sure these guys are ok," Larry said.

"Something good is happening," Phil added.

"I'm gonna head home, too," I said. "I'm not really tripping and it's been like six hours."

"You sure? Isn't it like a 45-minute drive?"

"Yeah, I should be fine though. It's late enough that no one will be on the road."

I said goodbye to everyone who was still outside and went to my car. I packed a bowl, and as I started driving, I started feeling like I was on mushrooms for the first time all night. It was like I was merging with the car as I pointed myself towards home. I could feel the ground under the tires, how the vehicle responded to my input. I hit the bowl, got out of Ted's neighborhood, and got on the highway.

XIX

"Maybe I shouldn't have left," I thought. "It's too late to turn back." I was on the highway driving exactly the speed limit and smoking a bowl at 2 am on mushrooms, which had started kicking in about six hours after eating them. It was the first moment I had been alone.

I could see a big arrow floating ahead of me, insisting that I drive on the shoulder of the road. A line of traffic cones was to my left to reinforce this point. "Is this really happening or am I just tripping?" I thought.

I found that slowing down made the shoulder feel less like a gravel road. The arrow grew closer and closer. Finally, I could see the electric arrow was mounted on the back of a truck that was repainting the lines on the road.

I let out a heavy sigh of relief and said out loud, "That would have been as confusing if I were stone-cold sober. And now I'm talking to myself. And can't stop. It's kinda weird," and I laughed and continued to smoke my bowl.

A few minutes later and I was off the highway and any road that cops routinely patrol. I got out my weed-filled dug-out, pressed in my one-hitter, and continued to chain smoke weed. I exhaled the smoke and said, "Just me and deer out here on this dark country road. Gotta be extra careful. Really trippin' now. It's beautiful out. The sky wasn't like this back at Ted's. Well, it was, but I couldn't see it. God damn, are those mountains? There's no way. They're clouds. Almost home. There's a deer... And another. Successfully avoided them. God damn it, I love this song… I hate what this world has become. This stretch of land would be so peaceful without this road and me lumbering through it in my noisy vehicle. Mine's not even that loud compared to some, but it's destroying the silence."

"You're right," the world responded.

I had read about, thought I had felt, and even discussed this with an inter-dimensional creature known as Raziel, but it was in this moment that I first saw myself not only as a human, but a part of nature, a part of the Earth, and a quiet, ineffable melancholy came over me as I saw what we as humans were doing to ourselves. I turned the music off and said, "One last turn and I'll be off this thickly wooded road and I'll have less chance of hitting a deer."

It felt like I was being magnetically pulled to go the way I was going. I couldn't have veered off course if I wanted to. I had been nervous about finding my way in the dark, as I hadn't lived around there, or driven, or made that specific drive, in almost a year. "All roads lead home," I said as I turned off one road and onto another. "There isn't anywhere where one road becomes another. It's one huge thing, stretching out across everywhere," I added.

I saw one last deer right before turning onto my street and I wanted to apologize to it.

Finally home, I stepped out of the car and was abruptly tripping much harder than I had been in the car. The mushrooms kicked in at full force and the sky exploded into my eyes, unfolding and stretching as far as I could see. I looked up and, out in my countryside home, took in the enormity of the sky, saw right through the sky to the stars, and all I could do was breathe.

I went to the front door and my big black cat was waiting to be let inside. I opened the unlocked door carefully so that I wouldn't wake the dogs.

I gave the cat some water, changed the water in my big

glass bong, topped it off with some ice, loaded the slide with weed, got a cup of water, went to my room, put on some music, and sat in my chair. The cat hopped onto my lap and started purring and kneading my leg with his little paws. The cat's fur felt so nice and he seemed so full of love. Looking at my new electric guitar, which my mom had kindly bought for me because the old guitar reminded me of May, I got out my notebook and started to write. "I hate this world but love what it has made. The electric guitar is a product of all that is wrong in the world but is one of my favorite things in the world. I love everything that I hate and nothing makes sense anymore." I took a hit from the bong, and continued, "When did this happen? When did things stop making sense? Mom is sick and could actually die. I believe Raziel when he says she'll be ok, but what the fuck even is Raziel? He's like some inter-dimensional hacker, accessing Rosa's sprite. How is that an experience I had, that other people had? I found a girl that I had dreamt of for years, who I had thought only existed in my mind. She meant everything to me and now it seems she will never speak to me again. Maybe she did only exist in my dreams? I found a group of people that I love and it's like our destinies are intertwined, we went through so much crazy shit together and just like that, we went our separate ways. Who knows when we will all be together again? I encountered actual evil. How can some-one like Don even live in this world? How could have any of those things actually have happened? And I somehow achieved all three of the life goals I set within a few months, but what happens after the credits roll?"

I took another bong rip and stroked the cat behind his ears. His ears looked so funny and his purring made me feel so good, the cat sounded so happy. I tried to think of the last time I felt like life honestly made sense, and then it hit me. "Nothing has ever made any sense! This isn't some new experience of life not making sense," I wrote, "I'm just noticing it for the first time! The veil has been lifted!" A wave of joy started spreading through me, from the crown of my head down my spine.

I reached for my leaf-bound notebook that I kept my magick stuff in and started to write. "I've been fooling myself all these years, thinking that I understand anything. Life is chaos! Why search for and try to create order that isn't there? Find peace in chaos, and all the questions end!" I put the notebook on the floor, and it felt like I had made it to the other side of the abyss. Looking down at the cat on my lap, with his goofy little ears, all I could do was laugh.

This page is left intentionally blank (in case you have some insight).

www.ingramcontent.com/pod-product-compliance
Lightning Source LLC
Chambersburg PA
CBHW030753110726
47900CB00008B/2581